The Last Thing You See: A New Adult Romance
Emma South

Published by Emma South

Copyright 2014 Emma South

Discover other titles by Emma South
at **www.emmasouth.com**

Disclaimer
All characters and events are entirely fictional and
any resemblances to persons living or dead and
circumstances are purely coincidental.

Chapter 1: Harper

"Harper! Can I have a photo?"

That's the danger with these meetings in public places, the ones that last long enough anyway, they'll always find you. I'd just stepped out of the café and hadn't even had time to put my sunglasses on before the first girl, who had been waiting patiently on the sidewalk for God only knew how long, wanted a picture with me. Normally I'd be happy to. I believed in giving as much back to my fans as I could. My career would be nowhere without them, after all. Today though, I wanted to let go of the carefully crafted public image and throw a tantrum. I wanted to fling myself to the ground, kicking and screaming like a child.

I put my sunglasses back in my handbag and smiled. "Sure!"

"Omigodomigodomigod! Thank you! I loved you in The Last Perfect Day!" she said.

The Last Perfect Day was an action-adventure-zombie-apocalypse movie that was a definite milestone in my career. Before that, people would always tentatively ask me if I used to be Princess Sundancer, or if I played Bella from The Wych Elm. After The Last Perfect Day, people would come up in the street and ask me if I was *Harper Bayliss*, and life was never the same.

"Aw! Thank you so much."

I leaned in close and we both looked at the camera held in her extended arm while my brother, Orson, hovered close by in case somebody got too grabby and my mother waited a bit farther back, engrossed in something she was reading on her smart phone. The camera made a little clicking sound and the girl turned it around to make sure it was a good shot before beaming at me so brightly I felt my rage go down a few notches. "Could you sign this?" her friend asked, holding out a photo of me in my Dark Fox outfit, a promotional shot for the movie-adaptation of the comic book, along with a felt pen. I took the pen and signed the photo as she held it.

"And this?" another girl held out a blank piece of paper.

"Sorry, that's enough, we've got to get going," my mother and de-facto manager called out.

My brother stepped in and gently guided me back in the direction of our car, much to the disappointment of the third girl. I wasn't supposed to sign blank pieces of paper anyway, in case somebody then printed some kind of contract onto it afterwards. It's a crazy world. "Sorry! Bye!" I called over my shoulder, thankful that the news about my location had only travelled as far as a few fans, not a bunch of paparazzi.

I reached back into my handbag and put the sunglasses on, big ones that covered a significant portion of my face. It was a surprisingly good disguise. My cloud of anger darkened again and I pulled out a bottle of water to suck back while I tried to collect my thoughts.

Mom tapped away at her little screen, seemingly oblivious to the daggers I was shooting at her from behind the sunglasses. The whole meeting, I'd tried to get a word in edgewise but I had been shushed and ignored, and now it looked like I was going to be signed up for a movie I had little enthusiasm for.

Orson walked slightly behind, earning his keep as a sort of bodyguard for me. At big events and at television studio interviews, where there were lots of people, we had to rely more heavily on the security of those event organizers and studios, but for the most part Orson was deterrent enough.

My mother had decided that full-time bodyguards were sometimes too heavy-handed and often only solved the extra problems that they themselves created. Besides, it was good for my brother to have a job, to be a cog in 'our little machine' and keep it all in the family.

"You should be able to read for that in June then," she said, apparently looking at my schedule.

"I don't want to be Estella." I said.

"It can't be *all* zombies and superheroes, honey," she said, as if that was even close to the truth or enough of a reason. "We're not having you typecast, not at this stage of your career. Don't be silly now."

My face burned at the phrase, the same one she'd used when I was a kid and didn't want to pick up my toys instead of a twenty-year-old woman talking about my own job. The role of Estella, a girl in Great Expectations by Charles Dickens, hit a little too close to home for me and I wished I could tell her why, but that was a conversation I feared more than the role itself.

"Besides, it's all done now. It's basically a formality, he wants you in and we've agreed. You don't want to get a reputation for being flaky in this business," she finished.

I sighed, feeling deflated, and looked up the sidewalk a little bit as the dry heat beat down on us. Standing in front of a restaurant, just outside the ropes that cordoned off an outdoor seating area, was somebody that looked like trouble if ever I'd seen it.

Head and shoulders over most of the people around him, I could already see the tattoos, the huge arms, and the scruffy clothing. If he was in one of my movies, he'd be a henchman for sure.

"Look out for that one," I said quietly to Orson, who nodded and moved in front and to my left so he would be between myself and the big guy when we walked past.

As we closed the distance I could see that he had plenty of scars too, all kinds of cuts on his arms as if somebody had tried to scribble out his tattoos with a knife. Violence, all kinds of bad things, probably followed this man wherever he went.

He looked up from some pamphlet in his hand, first straight across the sidewalk, and then at me. Right at me. Despite my misgivings, my heart fluttered. He had far too much presence for a mere henchman.

Under the stubble, the tattoos, and the scars, or maybe even *because* of them, was a hell of a handsome man. *Every girl needs a bad boy in her past*, I thought, and he could be my bad boy any day.

I dropped my gaze to the ground and fought back a goofy smile. Now I really *was* being silly. When I looked up again, I was sporting no more than a calm and collected Mona Lisa expression, but I kept my eyes on him from behind the privacy of my sunglasses. Only a few more steps and he'd be just some hot guy that I saw one time.

"*You made me do this, you bitch!*"

The scream came from the right, the road side of the sidewalk, and caught me completely off guard. I flinched and then froze on the spot as a man in a cheap-looking blue tracksuit rushed towards me with something in his hand.

Orson, who had been concentrating on the big guy almost as much as I had, was taken equally by surprise, hearing the yell but not where he expected trouble to come from. The world seemed to go into slow motion as I heard my mom gasp in fear, but I couldn't make myself react. I was a deer in the headlights.

A cup. It was some kind of cup in his hand and he was pulling it back as if he meant to throw it right at me. Was it coffee? Was he going to burn me?

Please don't burn me.

I would have sworn the liquid, clear not black, was flying through the air before anybody moved, but maybe I was wrong. Whatever it was, I was going to get drenched.

Moving faster than a man of his size had any business doing, the guy with the scars jumped in the way, taking a splash in the chest that would have hit me full in the face. Sparkling droplets of the liquid hung in the air and caught the sunlight like crystals before the world returned to normal speed.

The man in blue took off like a rocket and a few drops of the liquid, water presumably, landed on my forearm. The big guy who took the hit for me faltered as he recovered from his nearly headlong dive and then sprinted after the fleeing man.

I watched them go, feeling the cold grip of fear still squeezing my heart like a balloon it wanted to pop but wasn't quite able to. Something was stinging my arm and I looked down, expecting to see some kind of giant wasp there, but there was nothing like that, just the few droplets glistening there.

The pain quickly got worse, like these small beads of water were boiling hot or something, and I screamed as I pulled at the top of my water bottle and doused my arm. Still, however badly I was hurting, the man who saved me had it much worse.

Before he could catch up with the man in blue, I saw him stumble and then fall to the ground, screaming and pulling at his clothes, which looked to be literally *smoking* and melting off. Everybody was just *watching* as if this was some kind of street performance.

"Water!" I screamed.

Leaning over the rope in front of the restaurant, I grabbed a bucket off a table that had once held ice cubes and a bottle of wine but now held mostly water with a few tiny scraps of ice.

"Call an ambulance! Police!" I yelled at the closest person as I arrived and dumped the water on the writhing man. "Tell them it's acid!"

I went back for more water, bringing my hand to my mouth as I ran and tears of shock started flowing from my eyes. The noises he was making, so much pain being forced through a throat that sounded like it was almost clamped shut, I'd never heard anything like it. I never wanted to hear anything like it again.

Chapter 2: Harper

"How about on social media? Anything unusual been happening there lately? Threatening messages on Facebook or Twitter?"

The police detective had his notepad and pen at the ready and was fixing me with a disinterested expression, like he was working on a production line in a factory rather than investigating an acid attack on a Hollywood actress in the middle of L.A. If it weren't for the modern clothes, I would have expected him to be talking about dames and dive bars and to be smoking a cigarette to pass the time until he could get back to the whiskey in his office.

"I don't know, I don't think so. It's usually not me running my public accounts directly anymore, a couple years ago they just got too many people following them for me to handle, so we have Jenny, Jenny Wilson, to log in and post as me. My mom tells her what we want to put out there, Jenny writes the draft, and then my mom OKs it."

"Where can I find Jenny to speak to her?" he asked.

"Here are her contact details." My mom pushed her phone over the table, where the detective copied Jenny's details into his notepad.

"But there's like, a torrent of filth and threats that come in on those accounts, I already know that much. People ask me to come visit them in their countries and to make sure I come alone, others say they'll kill me because I didn't play Dark Fox right. There's just so much of it," I said.

"Mmmhmm," agreed Detective Ridley, "people tend to blow a lot of hot air on the Internet. I'm sure a lot of thirteen-year-old boys will piss their pants when I knock on the door and there'll be a lot of wild geese being chased, but I'll follow up on everything, I promise you that."

"How does somebody just disappear in the middle of the day like that? How did he not get caught already?" my mom asked.

"What probably happened was he had other clothes under that tracksuit, and he tore it off as he went around a corner before making his way to wherever his car was parked. As far as we've been able to find, he didn't drop the cup and he didn't ditch the tracksuit anywhere near where the incident took place, which obviously gives us less to work on. That was clever on his part but, on the other hand, he did this in an incredibly public place and that was pretty stupid. In my opinion, he's thought about what he was going to do a lot, but he's more than a little unhinged and desperate. He'll have made enough mistakes for us to catch him, I think."

"I hope you find him fast," said my mom, accepting her phone back from the detective.

Detective Ridley nodded. "That'll be all for now, if you can't think of anything else that might be relevant?"

I shrugged, my mom shook her head slowly, and the policeman flipped the cover back over on his notepad before standing up.

"Oh, one other thing," he said, "Maybe you should look into some kind of bodyguard, somebody more full-time than Orson."

"We'll definitely look into it," said my mom.

We both accompanied him to the front door, where he left us with a nod and a 'Mrs. Bayliss, Miss. Bayliss', before heading towards his car. The door clicked shut behind him and I rubbed at the bandage on my arm.

"How's it feeling, honey?" she asked.

"It doesn't hurt, just kind of itches a little bit every now and then."

"Is it going to… scar?"

I rolled my eyes and walked away. She was worried about my marketability. At a time like this.

"Harper? Where are you going? I asked you if it was going to scar."

My mother followed me to the kitchen, where I grabbed my car keys off the hook. When I turned around she was right there in front of me, a look of confusion on her face, and I took a deep breath to calm myself, grasping at the hope that I might have misjudged her.

"They said probably not, it was only a few drops and was washed off really quickly. That poor man, though. Nick. Nobody has told us what's going on with him, if he's going to be alright. He got hit by a lot more than I did. I'm going to the hospital to thank him."

"We can't go now, Harper, we've got to record an interview with Jay and Maria."

I gave her a blank look.

"For The Breakfast Show?" My mom held her hands out at the sides, palms up, in exasperation.

"I know who Jay and Maria are, Mom. We'll have to reschedule. It's been two days already and I haven't thanked him. He might have saved my *life*. Without him, there wouldn't be any more interviews, no more movies, no more anything."

"But… Pandora Rising isn't going to promote itself. I've already had flowers sent to his room. Don't be silly now."

"Flowers? *Flowers*? Did he look like somebody who cares much about flowers? Mom…"

The woman who raised me put her hands on her hips and gave me 'that look', the one that used to warn me how close I was to being grounded or having my phone taken away for a month. I felt so small next to her, even though we were the same height now.

I was a fraction of a second away from muttering 'OK', but then in my mind I heard the sounds Nick had made on the sidewalk. He took a bullet, of sorts, for me. How could I live with myself if I didn't even thank him?

I clenched my fists at my sides, one on my keys and the other on nothing, and forced myself to look her in the eye.

"I'm going."

*****

I didn't believe I had actually resisted my mother until I was safely parked in the hospital car park. I'd never done anything like such blatant in-your-face defiance in even my most rebellious teen moments.

But she had changed too. When things started getting *really* big, when the contracts started having that many zeroes in them, she changed.

Nobody had ever done more for me than her. Until two days ago. Maybe that was what gave me that last little bit of strength to get those words out and edge past her in the kitchen.

With my trusty sunglasses and a cap, I hoped for the best and made my way inside the hospital as quickly as I could. The lady behind the reception gave me the room number for Nick Martell along with a quizzical look, but I left before she could ask whether I was Harper Bayliss.

I walked down the corridor on the sixth floor, looking up at the numbers over the doors until I arrived outside room six dash eighteen, glad that everybody seemed more intent on rushing around with clipboards than looking at me. A sudden wave of nerves hit me as I took off my sunglasses and hat and stuffed them both into my handbag.

What if he was angry about what had happened to him? What do you say to somebody who's in the hospital because of you? I realized I should have thought about that before I arrived.

Still, I was here now. I ruffled my hand over my head to take care of the hat-hair and tentatively walked in. It was a room with just one bed in it, drab and clinical except for a single bouquet of flowers on a table by the window, which at least let in some bright sunshine to warm up the décor.

"Hello?" I said quietly.

Nick was asleep, with an oxygen mask over his nose and mouth, and apparently shirtless under the hospital sheets. His skin looked hot and red where the acid had burned him, further distorting tattoos that were already crisscrossed with scars from older cuts.

Even if I didn't get a lasting mark from my exposure to the acid, I couldn't imagine Nick would get away unscathed. Scars on top of his scars.

His muscles occasionally twitched and strained as he dreamed. His breathing, at times, came fast and ragged. It didn't look like a good dream.

I stood at the side of the bed and wondered what to do. How long could I wait here? Then the sleeping man did something I never would have expected from somebody who looked like him.

He was tall enough that he barely fit in the bed, muscular enough that he must work out every day. Some tattoos, like the one on his shoulder, looked like they might have something to do with the army. It was hard to tell with all the scars though.

He was crying. A lump rose in my throat and I reached out to hold his hand as I stood by his bed.

Chapter 3: Nick

It was so fucking cold. My neck hurt. Of course everything else hurt too, but that one was new. I must have fallen asleep in the chair.

My right eye was still swollen completely shut, but the swelling must have gone down enough overnight for me to make out a few details through the left. The sunlight was still orange and had not yet begun to blast down with the white heat of full day. It shone in through the hole in the wall they called a window. It was early. The problem was, he always started early. As if on cue, the door downstairs opened, and heavy footsteps climbed the stairs up towards the room I was being held in.

I had no idea where I was, no idea if anybody knew I was still alive. What I did know was that I was going to die here. The door burst open, the enthusiastic gesture of a man who really loves his work.

"Ah, good morning, Corporal Martell. I see you are awake. Maybe my training is doing you some good, my friend? Maybe it is making you to be not so lazy? Yes?"

I didn't answer, I had nothing left to say. He already knew everything I was ever going to tell him.

"We've got a big day today, my friend," he continued. "Time to get serious. Want to guess what's happening?"

I didn't know what he was talking about, but I could see him pulling those fingerless gloves out of his pocket and putting them on. If you're going to be punching somebody a lot, you want to be wearing gloves.

When he had strapped them on to his satisfaction and it didn't look like any response was forthcoming from me, he hit me with an arching right hook that came down square on my cheekbone. That ought to even things up, swelling wise, pretty soon.

"Nothing to say? Don't want to sing the Star-Spangled Banner for me? OK, because I like you so much, I'll tell you."

My 'friend' leaned in close until his mouth was right by my ear. The first day I found myself in this chair, I flinched because of his body odor. Now though, I couldn't smell a thing through the clotted blood in my nose, and even if I could, his aroma would now pale in comparison to my own.

"Today I'm going to take your feet off," he whispered. "But that is for later."

I was in and out of consciousness for much of the day. Sometimes I was being beaten, sometimes I was being cut. All the while, he spoke to me.

'My friend' this and 'my friend' that. By the time the day was stinking hot, I had a newly broken rib and every breath was like fire that wheezed out of me. But I was still in control.

I was just a tiny spark, walled up in the last little fortress of my mind. Despite all the pain, despite all the talk, he hadn't yet found a way inside. But then he did.

"Hey, my friend, you got somebody waiting for you back home? Maybe some pretty girl?"

I didn't want to react, I tried to ignore it, but I must have done something. Did I stop breathing for a moment? I didn't know, I was in no state to be in a poker tournament.

"Ah! You do! What's her name?"

Christie. Her face appeared before me in the darkness behind my swollen eyes. I'd been stopping myself from thinking of her. Those first couple of nights, after my friend was done for the day, I had thought about Christie, hoping it would make things easier. It hadn't. The idea that I'd held her for the last time, heard 'I love you' for the last time, had my last kiss, was too much. So I'd let myself live through one last memory, that day we had ice cream on the bench by the lake, and then I shut her out. But now she was back.

"Let me tell you this, the funeral will be what you call closed-casket for whatever pieces of you get sent back. She would vomit at the sight of you."

For the first time since I wound up in this place, I cried. The
tears managed to force themselves out through my puffy eyelids,
and I felt their salty sting on my cuts.

Only for a few seconds though, because my sobs were like sunshine
on this guy's solar panels, and the blows I couldn't see coming
started once more. Christie always could bring down my walls,
but I never thought it would be used against me.

"You will never see her again, my friend," he said during a water
break. "I promise you, I promise you, that the last thing you
see will be my smiling face."

Reality started to become a hazy concept. His voice and his
beating, the very pain that dominated my entire existence, took on
a distant quality, as if I was floating away from my body.
You got somebody waiting for you back home?
You got somebody waiting for you?
You got somebody?

*****

When I woke up, the light was so bright I could barely
see. Must have been somewhere near the middle of the
day, but it wasn't hot at all, it was crisp and cool.

The whole room was white and blue, not the dusty old
stone I expected. What happened? I made it out? This
wasn't the army hospital tent… I remembered that that
already happened too.

My eyes adjusted further and I saw that, even if it
wasn't the army tent I'd first woken up in after my
rescue, it was most definitely another hospital. I
struggled to clear my head as the memory of the
nightmare, the same old nightmare, still tried to hold on
to my mind.

And somebody was holding on to my hand. I turned
my head and then my eyes travelled up along a bare arm
to a face so perfect and somehow familiar that it only
served to increase my confusion.

Now I remembered the acid attack, coming to the hospital, and 'talking' to the police. I was supposed to be in L.A.

That nightmare always left my head all jumbled up. It was so vivid every time. Waking up to this made me think I must have died in that chair, because now there was an angel holding my hand.

Her hair was long and glamorous, falling in loose dark waves over her shoulders, framing a face that was looking down at me with such care and concern that I wanted to tell her I was OK just to put her mind at ease. I wanted to see her smile one of those smiles that go all the way into the eyes.

Her skin was flawless, normally the sign of a lot of make-up, but if that was the case here I couldn't tell, she looked like a natural beauty. She was maybe the most classically beautiful woman I'd ever seen in real life.

Athletic and so very feminine, I was physically drawn to her in a way that I hadn't experienced since Christie. Surely no man could look at her without feeling it, without wanting her.

For me, though, there couldn't be anybody after Christie. There just couldn't.

Chapter 4: Harper

Nick slowly opened his eyes and turned to look at me, his breaths coming much more calmly and quietly through the oxygen mask now. He didn't say anything, I didn't even know if he *could* speak, but under a thick blanket of confusion I thought I saw some kind of half-recognition.

There was more than that too. The quick glance down my body before returning to my eyes was so fast it probably wasn't a conscious decision on his part. Men might not think women notice that kind of thing, but we do.

I was perhaps more used to it than most, I was paraded around in front of a lot of people more often than most anyway. Sometimes it made me feel embarrassed, worried that I wouldn't stand up to the scrutiny.

Usually men seemed to like what they saw, but not always, and the unspoken rejections affected me more than they should have. When I slipped up and let myself read some of the things written about me, like yesterday when some random person wrote that the acid probably would have made an improvement to my looks, it didn't help my self-doubt.

Sometimes the most positive responses were the worst. Sometimes I couldn't tell if people could even see me behind the characters, behind the carefully crafted image. Sometimes I couldn't tell if they were just faking it for whatever reason.

With Nick, it felt like there was some kind of energy between us when our eyes met properly for the first time. I would have sworn on my life that he felt it too. His blue eyes lit up like the sky on a clear summer's day and I was lost for words.

Then they clouded over and he looked away again, and he pulled the sheet up to his chin with his other hand. It left me with butterflies in my stomach as if I'd been floating on air, realized that's not how people really walk, and then fell back down to earth.

I pulled my hand out of his, feeling suddenly awkward and unsure of that I'd read in his eyes. I looked down at my feet for a second, licking my lips and trying to think of what to say when he reached for a small whiteboard and marker that was resting on a table next to his bed.

After scribbling on it for a moment, he turned it around with a slow reluctance to reveal a question.

'Are you Harper Bayliss?'

"Yes. And you're Nick. The police told me."

Nick spun the whiteboard back around, quickly rubbing off the previous words with the side of his hand and writing something else there.

'Why are you here?'

"Um… well, I mean… sorry I didn't come sooner, if that's what you mean. I just wanted to come by and say thank you. You know."

I gestured at the small bandage on my forearm and then thought of the painful burns he had endured and felt my eyes watering. I didn't want anybody to be hurting because of me. Nick's next message was accompanied by an incredulous look.

'That was you?'

I nodded and threw my hands up for a moment before wiping my eyes. "I'm so sorry, Nick. That man was going to… you stopped him and now you're here because of me."

Nick shook his head and wrote a new message.

'Not your fault'

"I guess not. But still, I can't thank you enough. Can I… give you a hug?"

The moment I said it, I felt like a moron. Nick's eyebrows raised and he hadn't finished writing his next message, nor had my blush begun to fade, when his doctor cleared his throat from the doorway.

"That wouldn't be a great idea. Nick's skin is still extremely sensitive," he said.

"Is he going to be OK?" I asked.

Glancing down at the whiteboard, which Nick was now holding so only I could see it, I saw it read 'Rain check?' and couldn't help but feel the corners of my mouth lift in a tiny smile.

"Are you happy for me to speak with Harper about your injuries, Nick?" the doctor asked.

Nick gave a shrug and a thumbs-up.

"By the way, my daughter has dressed up as Princess Sundancer for the last three Halloweens, she's your biggest fan, Harper."

"Oh really? That's so cute! Thank you."

"Anyway. Mr. Martell here is going to be just fine. Thanks to the quick action of bystanders with all the water, the burns are not going to have any lasting effect beyond some scarring. The only reason he's still in here is because of the inhalation." The doctor waved his hand around his mouth, indicating the oxygen mask Nick was wearing.

"Oh, what's up with that?"

"Well, unfortunately, Nick inhaled some of the fumes and it's given him some minor burns down his trachea, the windpipe. It's resulted in some difficulty breathing and talking, but there's no evidence that there's been any damage to his lungs, so he's just here for observation. And the Jell-O, they all stay for the Jell-O."

'It is good'

The doctor chuckled at Nick's sign while Nick pulled a water bottle with a straw from some drink holder hooked on the side of his bed and held his mask out of the way while he drank a few good gulps.

"So I'm just doing my rounds, making sure you're feeling like you're on the mend. Are you?"

Nick gave another thumbs-up.

The doctor mimicked a large tick on an imaginary clipboard. "And sleep, did you manage to get some?"

'Some'

"OK, great. These kinds of injuries can make it incredibly difficult to get to sleep and stay asleep, so keep it up and you'll be out of here in no time."

"Thank goodness," I said.

"Well, I'll leave you to it... um."

The doctor was looking unsure of himself for the first time, like he was suddenly out of his element.

"Would you like me to sign something for your daughter? Or a photo, maybe?" I asked.

"Oh! Would you? That would give me some much needed street-cred. I've got my phone here." He pulled it out of his pocket.

"Hmmm. Actually, I've got an idea. Does it take video?"

"Yeah, what did you have in mind?"

"Just tell me what button to press, I think she'll like it. What's her name?"

"Her name is Kelly. You just tap here to start and then there again to stop."

I took the phone from him and pressed the icon on the screen where he had pointed, quickly turning it around to point at myself and holding it out at arms-length.

"Hi Kelly, I heard about your Halloween costumes and I wanted to say thank you! Listen to your dad, he's a good friend of mine. Don't forget the magic word and, whatever you do, never forget to dance."

I finished the video with my head resting on the shoulder of Kelly's dumbfounded-looking dad while I smiled my best fairy-princess smile. The doctor accepted his phone back as if it was a bar of solid gold and grinned at me.

"Thank you so much. With this, we might be able to stop tying her up to get her teeth brushed."

"That's alright. You know, anything I can do to help in the fight against tooth decay."

Nick snorted out a laugh that immediately turned into a coughing fit and only managed to get himself under control after another drink of water. He was left red-faced and breathing hard by the end of it and I found myself back by his bedside with a hand on his shoulder, an area unmarked by the burns, before I even thought about what I was doing.

"Well Nick, I was starting to think you weren't going to have any visitors, but I see you go for quality over quantity. Good plan. I'll see you later. Nice to meet you, Miss. Bayliss."

"Bye."

Once again, I retrieved my hand from Nick. It was odd that I couldn't seem to keep my hands off of him, surely it must have made him uncomfortable, but I guessed it was a bit too much effort to write it down.

I went over to the bouquet on the table by the window and looked at the little card tied to the stems. Just as I thought.

"So these flowers are from me," I said.

'Very nice'

"It's the first time I've seen them. My mom ordered them and said it would be enough, but I didn't think so."

Nick shrugged.

'Glad you came'

I smiled. "So, I... uh... cleared my schedule for an hour or so. Mind if I stay? Shoot the breeze a bit?"

Nick gestured to the chair next to his bed and I took it, putting my feet up on part of the frame under his mattress. I wasn't sure how well a conversation could flow under the circumstances, but we didn't do too badly.

I found out that Nick was a former Marine, discharged last year, and was now working security for Jeremy Holt, a local businessman who I knew actually lived on the same street as me. Small world.

None of his answers were quite what I had expected, given my first impression when I saw him on the sidewalk. Under that bad boy exterior he was totally different, though he did seem to avoid some questions and turn the conversation back to myself. Maybe that was just easier because I could actually talk.

Either way, there was something about him that was intriguing. It was more than the fluttery feelings I got when he looked me in the eye, but that didn't hurt either.

My time was running out though. I had a photo shoot to get to, one that would now probably have to consist of clever poses with one arm behind my back.

The thing was, I didn't want to say goodbye. There was something special about being close to him. It wasn't fair that somebody like that, somebody that did what he did, would only be part of my life for such a fleeting moment.

But where would he fit in? What would my mother say? Something along the lines of how bad for my image he would be, probably. Maybe she was right... but still.

"I've got to go, Nick. I'm so glad to have met you though. Thank you again. I can't say it enough. Goodbye."

'Goodbye'

I stood and began to walk out, reaching into my handbag for my sunglasses and cap, and then turned around before I was out the door.

"If there's anything I can do, you know, about the medical expenses or anything?"

Nick waved the suggestion away but wrote something on his whiteboard and paused a long time before turning it around, as if he was struggling with the decision to show me.

'Would you visit me again?'

The question took me by surprise, as did the burst of joy that filled me up for a second. Then I came back down to reality again. My schedule was absolutely jam-packed for the next few days, it wouldn't be easy. I probably couldn't make it. No, definitely not.

"Yes. I'll visit again."

Chapter 5: Harper

I couldn't get Nick out of my mind. Even if I had *wanted* to, it didn't help that the attack was all anybody was talking about, not only in interviews but everywhere else I went too. It was probably too much to hope for that hospital security was keeping the reporters away from him, but I hoped so anyway. Everybody kept asking me about how much of an ordeal it was, and if I was scared. I probably should have been frightened, my attacker was still out there after all, but I wasn't.

The image of the man coming at me with that cup *did* flash through my dreams a couple of times, but then I saw Nick and those eyes of his. The cool blue of them calmed me and I felt safe again.

I also had an interesting idea. A cunning plan to get to know him better and if things got a little physical, then so be it. Maybe there was a place in my life where he might fit in, maybe he was the missing piece of my puzzle.

I couldn't get away the next day, it was too hectic, but the day after was a different story. My brother had driven and accompanied me to an interview on a radio show and when I asked if I could maybe drop him off somewhere and take the car, he said he could get some friends to meet up for lunch. Wheels ahoy.

When I arrived back in Nick's room at the hospital, I was happy to see him without the oxygen mask, but I would have been lying to say I was glad for the hospital gown he was now wearing under the sheets. A goofy grin forced its way on to my face when he looked at me. Damn, he was hot.

"I'm back!"

"Hi, Harper." His voice was croaky but sounded mostly pain-free.

"It talks!"

"Getting there. Thanks for visiting again, you didn't have to do that. I don't know what I was thinking, you must be really busy," he said.

"Who, me? Nah. Besides, what's more important than visiting my favorite human shield?"

"Well, when you put it like that…"

"Seriously though, it's good to see you getting better so quickly. I don't know if I could have lived with myself if, well, you know."

"Well, like I said, it's not your fault some guy went nuts."

Nick paused to take a sip of his water and I glanced around the room, seeing that the only real splash of color was still the bouquet my mom sent, though it was already showing signs of wilting.

"Still only allowing the very highest quality visitors through? Or doesn't your family like to give flowers?" I asked.

One side of his mouth rose in a rueful smirk. "There's just nobody that would want to visit me, really. My parents are gone and I'm an only child. My buddy from the Marines, the one who got me the security job, he dropped by, but that's about it."

"Oh, sorry."

"It's OK, it happened a while ago now."

"No special someone?" I asked.

The way Nick's face dropped, I felt like if I hadn't managed to get my foot *all* the way into my mouth with the question about his family, I'd got that sucker down to the ankle with this one. I saw his jaw muscles working as he clenched them and stared down at the water bottle in his hand in tight-lipped silence for a few seconds.

"No," he finally forced out.

"So, when are you likely to get out of this place?" I asked, desperate to change the subject.

"Today, actually. They say they've observed enough, I'll get a prescription for some kind of cream or ointment or something and I'm good to go."

"That's great! Will you be able to work now?"

"Well, I'm not sure. I'll have to check with my buddy, but maybe not. I can probably stand around as a deterrent, but if something happens, I might not be as effective as I should be and that's likely to be a problem."

"Are you going to be OK for money?"

"Yeah, I've got enough tucked away, this was just a temp job anyway while I was passing through. You don't have to feel like you need to pay for anything, if that's what you mean," he said.

"Well, that's not *quite* what I meant, but I did have an idea yesterday. If you can't do your other work, you probably won't be able to do this right away either *but*, how about a job?"

"What? Like as a bodyguard?"

"No. I need some help with one of my movies."

"Princess Sundancer needs some new dance moves?"

I laughed. "No, it's the sequel for Dark Fox, I need to do some hand-to-hand combat training because this one is going to be a lot more physical. I figured with you having been in the army…"

"Marines."

"Sorry, yeah, Marines. I figured you might be able to help with my training. What do you say?"

"Um…"

"Like a couple of hours a week, starting in two or three weeks?"

Nick clasped his hands together in front of his mouth and let out a little 'hmm', his eyes looking first down and to the left and then back up to me as he pondered. His brows furrowed in worry about something before I heard him sigh and his hands went back to his lap.

"Please?" I asked.

"That actually sounds really interesting. I've trained a few people in Brazilian Jiu Jitsu before, and a couple hours a week I could easily fit around the other job, if I'm even working it again by then. I mean, it'd definitely take the financial edge off the time I'm away now."

"Is that a yes?"

"Yeah."

"Thank you!"

"Shouldn't I be thanking *you*?" he asked. "I'm the one that just got a job, aren't I?"

Maybe he *had* just gotten a job, but I still owed him a hell of a lot more than he owed me. I walked around to the side of his bed and stuck out my hand, which he shook after a moment. The warmth of him spread up my arm and I felt like I was glowing.

Chapter 6: Harper

Orson drove the car and I went over my notes. Every time I went out promoting a movie it felt like the questions were all the same. In a way, that was a good thing. It was easier to prepare for.

What was it like to work with a director like Christian Vicario? What was it like to work on screen with an actor like Lucas Collins? How are you the same or different to your character, Pandora? Variations of these questions were a given.

Now, even though technically I was promoting Pandora Rising, there were going to be a lot of questions about the attack, and about Nick too. Who was this man who came out of nowhere? What's his story?

People expected me to have the answers, but I didn't. All I had was a vague idea of what I *wanted* his story to be, and that wasn't something for me to be talking about on national television.

The thought of him was making it difficult to concentrate on the pieces of paper in front of me. I'd looked up some video clips of Brazilian Jiu Jitsu and some of those positions looked pretty intimate, to say the least. If I was having trouble now, how could I possibly focus when he was between my legs?

"So," Orson interrupted an inappropriate thought, "Mom told me you went to see that guy in the hospital."

"Nick. Yeah, I did. What did she say?"

"Well, you know Mom, it's not what she said but how she said it."

"And how was that?"

"She said this interview we're going to now is one that had to be rescheduled because you blew it off the other day, and she's raving about your reputation and how Jay and Maria won't schedule you again and blah, blah, blah," he said.

"Oh, come on. How can she be so heartless? Has she forgotten what he did already?"

"She's not heartless, you know she's got your best interests in mind. She's just very… driven."

I sighed. "Yeah. Yeah, I know, but it was the right thing to do."

"What was he like, really? You know, behind the things you've been saying in the interviews. He looked like a drug lord's enforcer on vacation."

"He did, didn't he? He really doesn't seem like that at all though. I don't know much more than what I've been saying to the press. Let's see… um… he's ex-military, only child, working security for Jeremy Holt, you know, that guy down the street?"

"The billionaire?"

"Yeah."

"Trust you to call Jeremy Holt 'that guy down the street'," he said.

"Well, he is. Nick seems like a really good guy, Orson. He's got a sense of humor, even though I get the impression he's been through some bad stuff with the Marines. There's something about him."

Orson gave me a sideways look before returning his eyes to the road and indicating a lane change. We were almost at the studio now.

"There's something about him? He's a really good guy? This is from the girl who described the most eligible bachelor in Hollywood as boring?"

"Lucas wanted a trophy more than a girlfriend, and he never would have loved me as much as he loved himself. I bet he'd sleep with a full-length mirror if not for the danger of circumcision."

Orson shook his head, at a loss for words apparently. "No, you're right," I continued, "he'd never be that rough with himself. I can't believe Mom organized for us to go to the Fans Choice Awards together. It feels like an arranged marriage."

"Mom knows what she's doing. It's good PR, rumors of a co-star romance and all that, not like being seen with somebody who looks like they'd steal the silverware. Besides, it's just one date, you'll get over it, right? Just like Mom will get over this one little thank-you-meeting you had with this Nick guy."

Orson pulled around the back of the studio and parked near where a small crowd of people were being restrained behind some red rope barriers by the studio's security. They weren't there specifically for me, but they knew this show interviewed a lot of so-called big names so the group was always small and changed from day-to-day.

"Yeah. About that. I've actually seen him twice now. And, don't tell Mom, but I've kinda offered him a job." Orson looked at me as if I'd grown a third arm from the middle of my forehead. From the crowd, I saw a few people pointing and whispering to each other, trying to make out who had just arrived.

"What job?" he asked.

"Some hand-to-hand combat training to help for Dark Fox Two."

"Mom is going to be shittin' kittens, Harper. Don't worry about *me* not telling her. All I want to know is when *you'll* tell her so I can be out of the blast radius. Las Vegas ought to be far enough."

"Any excuse, eh? I don't know, I'm working up to it. Maybe it's time Mom *did* push out a litter though, she's going too far with her micro-management lately."

Orson held up his hands. "You didn't tell me this, I'm not listening, I'll be at the MGM Grand for an unrelated reason. I tell you what though, if you were looking for a way to get under her skin, you definitely found it. You ready to do this interview or what?"

I shrugged and opened my door, stepping out onto a red carpet that the studio rolled out whenever it wasn't raining. Orson walked around the car and one of the security guys joined us to help usher me in.

"Harper!"

I looked over and saw a girl with a camera take a photo from behind the barrier. With my brother and the studio security guy flanking me, I walked along the barrier and did a bit of meet-and-greet with anybody there who wanted to have a quick chat, photo, or autograph.

"Ms. Bayliss, they're saying they really want to get you into make-up now," said the security guy with his finger gently touching his earpiece.

"OK. Bye everybody!" I waved.

A discordant cheering of farewells rang out from the more enthusiastic of the fans. I waved and smiled until I was escorted through the door. There'd be a lot more people waiting when I came out.

Chapter 7: Nick

I stepped off the bus and looked both ways to get my bearings before setting off in the direction of the high rise where Holt had his offices and where my friend, Johnny, always started his day bright and early. He'd be settling down to breakfast at his desk soon.

As I walked, my mind wandered back to what had happened over the last few days. Harper Bayliss. The woman I saved from the acid was Harper Bayliss. She came to the hospital and held my hand. The guys back in the corps would have shot me for being a liar if I walked in and told them that, aside from the fact that had been in the news of course.

There was something she stirred in me, something that was fighting to fly to her like she was a magnet. I'd felt it when I first opened my eyes and seen her there, but managed to fight it down.

I told myself to just give her some time, enough rope to hang herself with. I thought I'd see that there was nothing much behind her beauty. She was a smoking hot girl that had coasted on her good looks her whole life. She was probably a bitch.

As far as I could tell, I was dead wrong. The concern for me that I'd seen on her face was real. The way she conducted herself was so classy, considering she must be getting pulled in a million different directions at once.

All the doctors and nurses that checked in on me, at a suspiciously frequent rate while Harper was there, who wanted autographs or something else. She just gave and gave like she'd never run out of giving. The video she'd made for that doctor's daughter was awesome.

People were drawn to her like nothing I'd ever seen before. She said the hospital was like a sanctuary compared to some places. It was all perspective, I supposed.

She made me laugh. Of course that ended in a coughing fit where I thought a lung was going to come up, but she did it. Then she was standing next to me again, hand on my shoulder, with her perfect skin touching some of those ugly scars. Not the worst of them, though.

I didn't know what made me ask her to come back. I promised myself it wasn't just the fact that when she sat down and put her feet up on my bed in those short-shorts, her legs seemed to go on forever.

By the time she was halfway through her second visit, her voice sounding like music to my ears, I managed to put my finger on it and my heart sank. It was Christie, she *really* reminded me of Christie.

If Harper had gone to our school, and in the same year as us, she and Christie would have been best friends. Christie didn't have friends anymore though.

The loss hit me anew and put a damper on anything Harper might have been stirring in me. I told myself it was simple, that Harper was a blindingly sexy woman and I was still a living man so I wasn't immune to her allure, but there was just no getting over some things. That's all there was to it.

I'd work with her, I'd be professional, nothing else. Besides, what did I think would happen? Even in an ideal world where I was open to the possibility, somebody like Harper wouldn't look at me the way Christie used to. Nobody could.

The skyscraper, commonly known as the Holt Tower, was owned by Jeremy Holt, but most of the floors were leased out to other companies. It may have been the hub of everything he did, but his empire was grown by buying smaller businesses and making them bigger rather than growing in one spot. As such, his employees and operations were all over the world.

That was all induction-stuff my buddy Johnny took me through when he got me the job. He left the corps a couple of years before I did because of an injury, but he was smart enough to coordinate a security team like nobody's business, so his role was all about driving the desk these days.

When I knocked on the door and got the go ahead to come in, I saw him eating a greasy breakfast with steaming coffee in a Styrofoam cup. He wiped off his hands when he saw me and forced the last mouthful down.

"Hey, you're out! The hit man was supposed to get you while you were in a weakened state! Come in, come in, take a seat."

I shook his hand and sat down in one of the two seats on the opposite side of his desk while he turned down the volume on the flat screen mounted on his wall. Some breakfast show was listing where to expect delays due to breakdowns.

"So, speak up. How are you?"

"I'm good, man, I'm good. My throat's still a little sore, skin's still pretty damn tender, but no change in the doctors' opinions. No lasting damage beyond scarring," I said.

"That's good, I mean scars, what's the difference right?"

"Yeah. Sure."

"And Harper Bayliss," Johnny gave an appreciative whistle and leaned forward as if he was going to divulge a state secret. "I know you couldn't talk back at the hospital, but the guys are dying to know. Is she anywhere near as hot in real life as she is on TV?"

I leaned forward too. "She's all that and more." There was no need to get overly deep and meaningful with Johnny.

"Ah, you lucky bastard."

"Lucky? Man, there's got to be a better way than that." We both leaned back again.

"Yeah, like being a movie star. I heard she's doin' that guy in her new flick. What's his name?"

"I don't know. She came to see me again you know, in the hospital," I said.

"Oh yeah? She must be *really* thankful, you've gotta use that to your advantage."

"I'm going to be seeing a bit more of her…"

"There you go!"

"Not like that, man, not like that. It's actually something I wanted to talk to you about," I said.

"Me? What do I know about dating movie stars?"

I rubbed my eyes with the heels of my hands and took a deep breath. Sometimes it was hard work talking to the guys from the corps. When the chips were down, they knew how to switch to business mode and kick ass, but damned if they weren't still in high school the rest of the time.

"Once again, not dating. She had a job offer for me, doing some Brazilian Jiu Jitsu training, starting in a few weeks. It's not a lot of time, but I wanted to check with you to sort out what hours you might need me for around then so I can work around it," I said.

"A few weeks?" Johnny sucked some air in with a hiss, "Not gonna lie to you, man, there's probably not gonna be a lot of hours for you. I mostly needed you around to look tough while he was hosting some important clients over the past few weeks, but they're gone now."

"Ah. I see."

"But hey, you know I'll work you into the rotation where I can, and there's a bright side."

"What's that?"

"You'll have all the free time you need to work your magic on Harper."

I shook my head. "You sure you won't need me? A few more breakfasts like that and you'll be trapped in this office."

Johnny gave me the ol' stink eye. "Still kick your ass, *Corporal*. Besides, it wouldn't matter if I did. Watch this."

Johnny, who had outranked me as *Sergeant* John Hocker for all of one month before his career-ending injury, tapped at some keys on his keyboard and clicked on something with his mouse. The video on the wall-mounted screen changed to something obviously taken from a security camera, the display changing to a different camera every ten seconds or so.

"It's all connected," he said, waving his hands mysteriously as if there was some magic involved. "I can run it all from here."

"Pretty neat. This is all live?"

Johnny sipped his coffee and cleared away the remains of his breakfast. "Yep, this is. Got enough storage for footage going back six months though. Let me tell you, that'd make for a boring movie night."

The screen changed to the image of a car stopped in front of a gate that I recognized as being located at the Holt household. The driver was talking to the guard about something.

"Check this out, we just got this new toy." He clicked the mouse and a little label popped up over the car with a picture of an hourglass in it, indicating that something was loading.

After about a second, the label filled up with a driver's license style picture of Jeremy Holt's driver, Stan, along with his full name and address and details of his vehicle. As we watched, another car drove by, a similar label attached to it appearing to float along.

"How does a civilian security system have access to this kind of thing?" I asked.

"One of Holt's companies designed the software, and we're testing it. Pretty good stuff, huh?"

"It's a fantastic command center, sir."

"That's more like it."

Johnny tapped a few keys, clicked the mouse, and the display changed back to the breakfast show, but my heart nearly jumped into my throat when Harper's face came on screen in high definition. In the background behind her was a promotional image of some movie called Pandora Rising.

"There's your girl," said Johnny, bringing up the volume.

"Not my girl," I muttered to deaf ears.

"Not so much at the time," Harper was saying to the hosts of the show, "I thought it was a hot drink or something at first, which would have been bad, but after it sunk in that it was acid... *acid*... and I, you know, processed what it did to the man who jumped in the way. Yeah. It was scary."

"Have you spoken to this man since?" asked the hostess, who I guessed was probably Maria rather than Jay, if the logo at the bottom of the screen was anything to go by.

"Yes, I have. The good news is that he's going to be OK."

"Wow, that's a relief. How do you even think of what to say to somebody who did that?" asked Jay.

"Yeah, I know. It was a humbling experience. I mean, here I am, just a girl who pretends to be fictional characters for a living. Today I'm a princess, tomorrow I'm a superhero. Then I meet a real superhero." Harper took a shuddering breath and her eyes looked all glassy as she put a hand to her upper chest, swallowed and blinked a few times. She inhaled deeply and let it out slowly before continuing.

"Sorry. He's… just… he's just my hero. And he was a hero before he saved me too, he was in the Marines, you know. I'm so grateful. I can't even…" Harper threw her hands up in defeat.

"Well, so are we," said Maria, "and so are all your fans. Thanks for coming in, Harper, always so nice to see you." She turned to the camera. "Pandora Rising, starring Harper Bayliss and Lucas Collins, opens in theatres across the country next Friday. Make sure you go see it. Here's an exclusive clip."

"Lucas Collins, that's the guy," said Johnny.

Chapter 8: Harper

I managed to get from my car to the gym Nick had chosen without being seen, as far as I could tell. It had a room with padded mats on the floor that he said was suitable for the kind of training he had in mind. After contacting the owner, I was able to hire out the room for our sessions. Privacy was essential.

Nick was sitting in a small reception area just to the right of the door and threw down a magazine he had been browsing when he spotted me. He picked up a big sports bag and slung it over his shoulder as he stood.

The t-shirt he was wearing was just a little on the tight side, and the arm holes stretched around his biceps when he flexed them to sling that strap on. I hadn't seen him standing up since I'd first spotted him on the sidewalk, and I was struck again at just how imposing he was. It took no small amount of willpower to not lick my lips.

"Hi! Wow, look at you! Looks like you're moving pretty freely."

"Yeah, I just gotta keep the burns out of the sun for a while longer. How have you been?"

"Good. Busy. Pandora Rising did better than expected, so I've been booked solid with extra promo to keep the momentum up as much as possible." I shrugged.

"Good problem to have."

"Yeah it is."

"You ready to get started?" he asked.

"Sure, which way?"

"It's up those stairs over there."

I walked ahead up the stairs with Nick following behind and soon found myself in a rectangular room maybe forty by fifty feet with permanent mats in a rectangular configuration right in the middle. Nick unslung his bag and knelt by it on the floor, taking out a couple of plastic-wrapped bundles and handing them to me.

"What are these?"

"This is your gi. We'll be doing most of your training in it."

I wrestled with the plastic and eventually uncovered a pair of white pants that had the same kind of feel as jeans, but with a drawstring, and a heavy white jacket made from similar material, which had a Brazilian flag on the left breast and some incomprehensible logo on the back.

We went to our respective changing rooms to get ready and then met back in the center of the mats. Nick was wearing a gi in the same style as myself but appeared to be wearing a rash vest of some kind underneath, whereas I had nothing but a sports bra under the jacket. My face maintained perfect innocence when I saw him glance down my body, the lapels of my jacket were open enough to show a *bit* of skin after all. Nick looked back up and smiled, and that broke my concentration enough that I smiled back.

"Your belt is tied up wrong," he said.

"It is?"

"Yeah, a knot like that sticks out too much, and when you're down on the ground it can dig in and be uncomfortable. The ends are too long and loose, not to mention it'll probably come undone a lot. Of course belts are always coming undone when you roll."

"Roll?"

"When you spar."

"Oh."

"Here, this is how it's done."

Nick tugged at my white belt and undid the simple knot I had tied and then moved behind me with the belt in his hands. Was he putting the moves on me? I turned my head to the left and kept him just in the corner of my eye. Was this the Brazilian Jiu Jitsu equivalent of the chivalrous man helping the love interest with her pool shot or her golf swing?

"Left side over right," he said.

"Huh?"

"Your jacket, left side over the right side, nice and tight."

"Oh, right."

My jacket hung loose without the belt to hold it closed and I pulled the right side over my torso before pulling the left side over the top of it. Nick lifted the belt over my head from behind and brought it down to waist-level.

"OK, watch. You pull both sides around the back and then to the front again, the belt goes around twice, see?"

"Yeah."

Nick was close behind me and I leaned back an inch or so, feeling the rear of my shoulders touch his chest as he bent down to tie my belt. My eyes were on my belt, but my mind was on him.

He showed me how to tie the belt and then stood back and got me to do it by myself. I looked at my knot, then at his, and saw they looked more or less alike.

"You're not a black belt?" I asked.

"Excellent observation. Purple." He pointed at the purple belt.

"What does purple belt mean?"

"It means I can beat most of the blue belts."

"I... see. You don't have to be a black belt to train people?"

"Nope. Don't get me wrong, they'd be better, but I trained people when I was a blue belt. It goes white, blue, purple, brown, black. It's not like some other martial arts where you get your next belt because you've punched through a hundred pieces of plywood, then two hundred, and so on. You generally progress by beating the majority of other people in your weight and belt-level in tournaments."

"I don't think I'm going to be entering any tournaments," I said.

"No, I didn't think so, but that doesn't matter. I thought what we'd do is get a good grounding in the basics, and then I'll show you a few moves that might look pretty cool on the big screen. Let's get warmed up."

If Nick *was* unqualified to be an instructor, it was certainly beyond my ability to tell the difference. The first hour of our session was essentially a cardio workout, starting with a few minutes of running around the perimeter of the mats, all kinds of different abdominal workouts, and drills of certain movements that were apparently pretty common in Brazilian Jiu Jitsu, or 'BJJ' as he referred to it.

Finally, after 'snaking' along the length of the mats I don't even know how many times and the 'upa' drill, he showed me a couple of techniques and we practiced them until our time was up. From my position flat on my back, a sweat-soaked mess, I knew I *wanted* to stand, but it was easier said than done.

Nick extended his hand and helped me to my feet. I hunched over with my hands on my knees, feeling like the temperature in the gym was somewhere around a million degrees.

"Oh my God," I breathed.

"You did really well," he said. "Your fitness levels are right up there, you could join the Marines."

I looked up, glad to see that he was at least as sweaty as I was, and managed to stand straight again. Transferring my hands to my hips, I pretended to ponder the idea.

"Hmm. No. Must get changed. See you out here in a bit," I wheezed.

I hobbled to the changing room and shrugged off my jacket. It was a heavy jacket to begin with and, going by the sloppy thud it made when it hit the floor, I judged it had doubled in weight due to my perspiration. I emptied my water bottle and then filled it up in the sink before slumping on a bench and getting halfway through it again.

The changing room had a couple of showers. I pulled out my shampoo and conditioner and then carefully adjusted the water temperature as cool as I could stand it. By the time I stepped back into the room with the mats in it, I felt mostly human again. Nick was waiting for me.

"So I'll see you again same time next week? You've booked it all, haven't you?" he asked.

"Yeah, I've booked it. But, um, I was wondering…" Suddenly I felt tongue-tied, and it took me a second to realize why. Any guy I'd been remotely interested in had always made the first move. The first obvious one, anyway. I was more than a little interested in Nick, but I was breaking new ground for myself here.

"What is it?" he asked.

"Um. I know a place pretty close to here, and they make a mean smoothie. I was wondering if you'd like to have a smoothie. With me. Hot day and all." I was thankful I was still flushed from the BJJ session and shower.

"Well…"

Nick dragged the word out and I felt weighted down with the crushing certainty that he was going to decline. I remembered when he first woke up in the hospital, the way his eyes shone for a moment, then that clouding over, the shutting down. Maybe I had imagined that first spark and just saw what I wanted to see.

"Yeah. I'd like to have a smoothie with you. My treat though, OK?" he said.

The weight came off in an instant and I felt buoyed. I didn't know where the energy came from, but I was smiling so wide I thought my cheek muscles would be as sore as any other by the end of the day.

"OK."

Chapter 9: Nick

Keep it professional. That's what I said I'd do, and I would, but holy hell, every moment with Harper made me wish more than anything that things were different, made me wish I could let myself feel that way again. It was like she had no idea about the kind of effect she had on people. On me, at least. The image of her lying on the mat, the jacket of her gi hanging loose and showing off her flat, glistening navel as she panted at me with half-closed eyes would stay with me forever. Then she came out of the changing room looking fresh as a daisy, if a little on the flushed side, and asked me to have a smoothie with her. I had to remember she was Harper Bayliss, too good for the likes of me, and this wasn't what it might look like to the casual observer. She was just being nice, being friendly. She was grateful to me, sure, because I happened to be at the right place at the right time. It was nothing more than that.

I could see why Harper would like this place. In addition to lots of outdoor seating for people to enjoy their smoothies in the sunshine, there were also several surprisingly secluded and private booths inside.

After telling me the name of the smoothie she wanted, stressing she wanted it large, she made a beeline for the side of one of the booths that gave the fewest people possible an angle to see her. I brought the smoothies back and slid into the booth opposite her, pushing her cup across the table.

I could have watched her suck on the straw and say 'Mmm' all day, but I made my eyes wander around the smoothie bar a bit instead. There was only so much a guy could take.

"So what was it like being in the Marines?" she asked.

"It had its moments, you know, highs and lows. I don't know what to say, most of the time was spent training, keeping fit and waiting, and then short bursts of the shit hitting the fan. No offence."

"Don't worry about me, I've heard worse."

At the counter, a drag queen nearly as tall as me, taller if you measured to the top of his-or-her fluorescent green peacock feathers, was ordering a smoothie and flirting flamboyantly with the uncomfortable-looking employee. I wondered if Harper was glad for something so eye-catching to draw people's attention anywhere but to her as we watched the young man's predicament.

"I can't tell you when I get off, company policy," said the cashier.

"I'll tell you when you *can* get off... " Began the drag queen before Harper started talking again and I couldn't hear any more.

"Get much of that in the Marines?" she asked.

"You're not allowed to modify the uniform like that," I said.

"No room for personal expression, huh?"

"Well... it's not so much about personal expression as it is about not going out in the field dressed like a bright green bull's-eye in a sequined bikini."

Harper laughed. "I suppose that's a decent reason for the uniform rules. So, no gay Marines then?"

"Well, there was *one* that I knew of. Sex Change Steve, that's what we called him. He was a badass when we needed him to be, but off duty he had some, uh, identity issues. He was sort of like one of those I'm-Not-Gay-But-I-Am-A-Woman-Trapped-In-A-Man's-Body types. Only it was a hell of a lot more complicated than that."

"Wow. How does it get more complicated than that?"

"Well, he was married for a start. To a woman."

"Oh! Like a marriage of convenience?"

"Nope." I shook my head.

"She didn't know?"

"There's 'not knowing' and then there's the degree to which his wife didn't know," I said, holding my hand out flat at one level and then raising it much higher. Harper sucked on her straw and then licked her lips before leaning forwards across the table.

"How deep does this rabbit hole go?" she asked.

"All the way, Harper. Get this, OK, he wasn't gay in any run of the mill sense of the word. He believed that his, uh… what did he call it… oh yeah, his 'true self' was a lesbian."

"He told you all this?" Harper said with disbelief written all over her face.

"Oh yeah, he was a buddy of mine. For some reason he thought I'd have some good advice for him on the topic. I don't know why."

"Well, did you?"

"Um… well, I said words to him. I don't know whether it was advice. Or good."

Harper laughed and rested her forehead on her hand for a moment, her elbow propped on the table as her shoulders shook with the giggles. When she looked up again, her dark eyes had a heart-melting sparkle to them.

"Oh my goodness. What did you tell him?" she asked.

"He had this whole plan, right? When he got home he was going to have a sex change, hence, Sex Change Steve. However, he saw no reason to consult with his wife before he did this."

Harper's jaw dropped.

"So I remember when he came to me with this question about the operation and I thought it was so obvious that I must have misunderstood. He asked me if I thought his wife would notice."

Harper laughed until she had no more air left to laugh with and twisted to the side to face the wall, away from any prying eyes in the smoothie bar, so she could double over. For a moment all I could see was her back, her hair, and her white-knuckled grip on the table as she cracked up.

When she came back up again there were streaks of tears running down her face and when she tried to talk, the words were broken up with snorts and giggles.

"So, like, they're in bed and she takes off his clothes… to see… to see a vagina and he thinks she's going to be like 'this all seems normal'?"

I thought back to my reaction at the time and laughed along with her. "Yeah, that's what I thought, but apparently that's not quite what he meant. Um, what he was really wondering about was if she would, and I quote, 'notice that he was becoming more beautiful'."

Harper shook her head. "What do you say to that?"

"What *can* you say? I dug deep, I got all philosophical on him. I said, Steve, a man marries a woman hoping that she'll never change, but a woman marries a man hoping that he *will*. So, I think she's going to be about as pleased as punch."

The two of us laughed, Harper fighting to swallow rather than spit out her sip of smoothie at first, and then spluttering out some hybrid cough-giggle. Then she reached across the table and touched my arm, and the contact was like a jolt of electricity.

It only lasted a moment, but it was long enough to remind me about who she was and who I was. It was enough for me to check myself.

I picked up my smoothie and took a big gulp as Harper congratulated me on my deep thinking. How she managed to get me talking so openly like that I didn't know, but talking to her had seemed like the most natural thing in the world to do.

Chapter 10: Nick

Harper soaked up BJJ techniques like a sponge, and I hadn't been kidding when I told her she was fit enough to be a Marine. It's always tough when you do a new kind of exercise, like maybe you can run marathons and then when you get on a bike you can barely even do the same distance, but after a couple more sessions, Harper never seemed to reach that same level of fatigue as the first day.

Each week there was nothing I looked forward to more than rolling with Harper and when she suggested we go for another drink afterwards, I happily agreed. With the amount she was paying me for lessons, it was only fair that I covered the cost of the smoothies.

She always got the same flavor, some dark green sludge called Biopure Rejuvenate that had lime, wheatgrass, and celery, among other things. I changed my order every visit, trying to find one I liked the best.

With an orange-colored smoothie in my left hand and green in my right, I joined Harper in 'our' booth.

"What made you join up?" she asked.

"The Marines?"

Harper nodded, pulling her drink over to her side. There were a couple of reasons. I decided to go with the one that was easiest to explain. "My dad," I said, "he was career military and always thought I should do the same. The Marines just so happened to have the closest office where I could sign up."

"But now you're discharged?"

I sucked some tasty orange, banana, and mango flavored smoothie through my straw and licked my lips, trying to think of how to steer this conversation away from the territory she was heading to.

"Yeah, last year. You were right, the smoothies here are awesome and I think I've found my flavor."

"Hey, this is my hometown, I know a thing or two," she said.

"Quite the hometown. You've always lived here?" Harper paused to take another pull on her straw, and her eyes never left mine. They were a soft brown that looked so warm, so kind, that they looked out of place in a big city like this, where everybody always seemed to be clawing at each other to make their own way to the top.

I'd seen and done some awful things, the worst that war can show a man. I'd faced a lot and been able to keep on marching, because I had to, but the way Harper looked at me made me feel weak in the knees like nothing else.

She swallowed and sighed, a flicker of some emotion crossing her face like an unwelcome memory.

"Born and raised," she said. "How about you? You're 'just passing through', so where are you really from?"

"A small town called Warfields in Missouri. The kind of town where nothing ever happens," I said ruefully.

"Warfields?"

"Yeah, named because of something that happened during the Civil war. I don't know, I didn't pay as much attention as I should have in that class. On the bright side, it was all over by the time I was born. So that's good."

Harper smiled and stirred her straw around in her rapidly depleting smoothie before looking up at me again. I wished the butterflies would settle down in my stomach.

"So why end the career?" she asked.

That did it, the butterflies were dead, but she continued anyway.

"I mean, you're obviously able-bodied. I've *rolled* with you now, and I thought *I* was in shape. I've seen you move at, like, lightning speed to be my hero and…"

"You need to stop. I'm not… comfortable with you calling me that. That's not me, I'm just some fuck-up who was in the right place that day. I'm glad you didn't get hurt, but that's not what I am."

Harper was silent for a while, taken aback by my unexpected little outburst. I felt like the worst person in the world to have just wiped that beautiful smile off her face. I expected she would make her excuses, leave, and that would be the end of my association with Hollywood's favorite starlet.

Not for the first time, Harper surprised me. "Was it a… what do you call it? *Dishonorable* discharge?"

"No. It was something else. You don't want to hear about things like that."

"Maybe. But, Nick…"

Harper reached across the table and her hand, chilled from holding her smoothie, slid into mine and gave it a squeeze. Compared to me, Harper was downright delicate. I was a bull and she was a china shop, but in that moment she felt so much stronger.

"Have you ever talked about it? Maybe you need to talk about it more than I don't want to hear it. I'm a good listener," she added tentatively.

If I looked up and saw Harper's face, I knew I'd probably do anything she wanted me to. I forced myself to stare at her hand in mine instead, but I faltered. I glanced up and there she was.

There was concern, but none of the pity I feared most. I was right about looking up though, Harper brought my walls down as well as Christie ever had, and everything started bubbling treacherously close to the surface.

"I was captured," I said. "That's where most of these scars came from."

Harper said nothing, she just waited for whatever was going to spill out as if her eyes were deep enough that all my pain could get lost in there and never find its way back. Her thumb gently stroked the back of my hand and I told her more.

I told her how even now I wasn't sure how it happened. Something exploded, my friends were getting shot to shit all around me. A bullet grazed me, something hit me in the head, and it all went black.

I woke up tied to a chair in some dusty little room, the chair itself secured to the stone wall by bolts. That's when I met the man who I thought was going to kill me. He said he would, and I had no reason to think he was bluffing.

He said that he wasn't officially part of any government or army, but the local insurgents 'fed' him foreign soldiers to torture. He was supposed to let some of them go so the word would spread that we should stay out of their war... or else.

The only reason he told me all that was because I wasn't going to be one of the soldiers that got released. He was going to have some fun and only my mangled corpse would ever be found.

He cut me, beat me, shocked me, made me loathe consciousness, and he enjoyed his work. But he didn't break me. Not until the last day.

I felt myself go pale when I thought about the last day, how he finally managed to get under my skin. My jaw muscles cramped and shut the words in so tightly that even Harper's presence couldn't drag them out, and I went silent apart from the wavering breaths that I managed to suck in through my teeth.

I shut my eyes when I felt them stung by tears, but that didn't stop them. They forced their way through and flowed down my face as fast as I could wipe them away. My heart felt like it was cramped and every breath was painful, as if the truth was going to make me explode like a pressure cooker. How could I say it?

When I was in that hellhole, when I was sure I would never reach out and touch Christie again, I shut her out of my mind. Then he used her against me, brought down my defenses and promised to give me enough scars to make sure that whatever got sent back home was an unlovable monster.

He may not have been able to work on me for as long as he wanted, but he did plenty. I saw the way people looked at me when I didn't cover up enough. I heard the whispers.

Harper stood and walked around the side of the booth, not letting go of my hand until she was right beside me, and she pulled me into an embrace, stroking my hair and shutting the world out. Her breasts pressed into the side of my head, soft and comforting under her shirt and bra, and I felt that clenching sensation in my chest begin to ease, the power to the pressure cooker turned off.

"I can't…"

"Shhh," she said, "enough. Just breathe."

It was good advice.

Chapter 11: Harper

Nick didn't want to be called a hero, but that didn't mean he wasn't one. To go through what he did and still be strong enough to get up every day was amazing. Over the next several weeks, he eventually managed to tell me how he got rescued. The little outpost he was being tortured in was raided and they found him there. It wasn't a rescue mission. They didn't know he was there until they stumbled across him.

He recovered, physically, but couldn't go back into service, so he was discharged. Every time I went to BJJ training with him and I saw the scars on his arms, or his rash vest rode up and I saw the scars on his stomach, I saw his strength.

I wanted to run my fingers over his whole body, trace every scar as if that would undo the pain that each one had caused him. As we rolled, I felt his muscles flex and I found myself with my hand inside his jacket more than the techniques strictly required, wishing he would forget the rash vest just once, but he never did.

Nick looked more relaxed every week, like a river that had been threatening to burst its banks but was now flowing nice and calm. His jokes came more often, his laughter easier, and it was infectious.

He was a gentle giant, probably strong enough to snap me like a twig, but I never felt safer than when I was with him. I knew the lengths he would go to, to stop me from being hurt.

One week, the owner of the gym couldn't let me book the room for our usual session. He had some special guest instructor coming in, so we had to come in a few hours later. It was full dark by the time we finished, but that didn't stop us from grabbing a smoothie, a tradition by that time.

Nick was almost all the way to our usual booth when I stopped him. "I've got an idea. Want to see something?"

He looked at me suspiciously. "Can my smoothie come?"

"Ugh. OK, yes, if it must."

"Alright then. Where are we going?"

"You'll see."

*****

Nick stayed in the car while I walked to the gate and put my key in the padlock, swinging it open so I could drive the car through. I paused on the other side. "Could you close the gate? Don't lock it, I'm just going to park over there."

After I parked, I grabbed the remnants of my smoothie out of the drink holder and stepped out. The city lights were laid out in front of me as far as the ocean and, by some miracle of meteorology, the stars were somewhat visible above too. I was just climbing onto the hood of the car when Nick returned.

"What is this place called?" he asked.

"It's the Hollywood Bowl Overlook. These ten parking spaces service the million cars that try to park here at any given moment during the normal opening hours. It's a busy place, but it closes at nine, and I like it best after dark anyway. I haven't been up here in... I don't even know how long now. I liked to come here alone, but since things got so crazy that's not such a good idea anymore."

"You want me to go stand guard at the gate or something?"

"No, I want you to climb on the hood and watch the city with me," I said.

Nick circled around and gingerly climbed on the hood of my car, easing himself down so as not to put a dent in it and finally relaxing against the windscreen like me, hands clasped over his stomach. I sighed contentedly, the glow from the latest BJJ workout making me feel snuggly warm.

The city, normally so loud and in-your-face, was utterly beautiful when it was reduced to lights in the darkness. It had been too long since I'd been up here. I didn't realize how much I had missed it.

Out of the corner of my eye I could see Nick soaking it all in, seeming to appreciate the serenity as much as I did. It was a comfortable silence where I let my mind wander, meandering from thought to thought as if looking for an old friend. Wary of old enemies.

Eventually Nick spoke. "How did you get a key to this place?"

"Hey, I told you this was my hometown. I know some people who know some people. I never brought anybody here before though."

"It's awesome. I love how quiet it is. You can see the whole city, and yet it's quiet."

I let that sink in for a while before turning my head to look at him. "Does it ever get any less scary? Those memories of being trapped? Hurt?"

Nick's eyes dropped from the city to his hands in front of him, where his thumbs tapped together for several seconds before he replied. "It has, lately."

"I wish I could stop being scared," I said.

"About the psycho with the acid? The police still got nothing?"

"No, it's not that. I mean, yeah, they got nothing, but... it's..."

Nick looked over at me, one eyebrow slightly raised, having picked up something from my tone of voice. Now it was my turn to look down. A lump rose in my throat and I tried to swallow it away, but it stayed put. Every time I took in a breath I opened my mouth to start speaking, but nothing seemed like the right way to begin. I must have done it half a dozen times before Nick spoke.

"Did somebody hurt you, Harper?"

"No. Sort of."

"What are you scared of?" he asked quietly.

"I'm scared that this," I waved my hand in the general direction of the city, then at myself, trying to encompass everything that my life was in one quick gesture, "isn't real."

Nick's brow furrowed and his eyes shifted sideways towards the city lights before coming back to me. "What do you mean?"

"Did you know I'm adopted?"

"No."

"You didn't Google me?" I asked, forcing as much mock indignation as I could under the circumstances.

"No."

"Well, I am. The information is out there on the Internet, but for some reason it's one of those things that never really piqued public interest much. You can never decide what the media will latch on to," I said.

"I guess not."

"Do you know what my first memory is? Like the first thing I remember that I *know* happened?"

"What?"

"It's not a birthday party. It's not a trip to the playground. It's not Mommy telling me she loves me."

I shut my eyes, and then really squeezed them as a full-body clench seemed to force the tears out, picturing that day when I was standing there in the middle of a puddle of juice with broken glass strewn through it. That woman with the hair pulled back in the harsh bun was leaning over me, so angry.

"Tipton Group Home. I spent a couple years in one of those group homes, the heir-apparent to those old-style orphanages, and this must have happened when I was around three years old. I can't really remember what happened just before this, but I remember dropping a glass of juice and it smashed on the floor. This woman who worked there at the time, nobody ever seemed to stay for long, rushed over and yelled something and I just started crying. I guess I must have pissed her off before or something. Then I remember…"

A sob shook my body as all the old fear, the *horror*, of the memory hit me again. My throat became a wary border control agent for words, taking every ounce of effort I had to force them through between each hitching breath.

"I remember she… she said… she just looked at me and said… she said…"

"Harper. Just breathe."

Nick was turned on his side facing me, his hand resting on the hood of the car between us to steady himself. I grabbed it like a life preserver and sat up, turning my body around to face him and eventually slowing my breathing to the same pace as his.

"She looked at me and said 'No wonder your parents didn't want you'. *That's* my first memory."

The eye of the storm passed, and I burst into uncontrollable sobs again until Nick pulled me into a hug and I cried myself empty right there on the hood of my car. By the time I was done, I felt dizzy like I was mildly drunk without any of the upsides. My head was resting in the crook of his arm and his other hand was carefully stroking my hair, tucking errant strands behind my ear when the breeze tore them free.

"That's the first thing I knew about myself. I was trash, so bad my own parents didn't even want me. All the other kids I knew in the home got chosen by adoptive parents before me, and by the time the Bayliss family came along, I literally didn't know anybody at all. I don't know what they saw in me, I just sat there not even speaking when they first visited. I didn't know what laughing was."

"Harper, you're..."

"I was so grateful to them for getting me out of there, but it sticks with you, you know?"

"I know."

"So a few years go by and, hey, why not audition for Princess Sundancer? They're remaking this movie that flopped a while back, what's the worst that can happen? Every seven-year-old girl wants to be a fairy princess, right?"

"That's my understanding," said Nick.

"So I get the role, and I remember thinking 'has the director gone crazy?' I haven't even had any acting lessons yet, but with my two years of ballet, the director thinks I have the right look to pull off the fairy princess who gets cursed by a witch and forgets the magic word and forgets the magic dance that makes the sun shine on the kingdom."

"Kazoosh!" said Nick.

"Ah, you saw it?"

"A long time ago now, yeah."

"The magic word was supposed to be 'Rizam!' but I came up with my own magic word and the director liked it better," I said.

"Rizam? Blech."

"Then the movie does alright, way better than the critics predicted anyway. I got a few more parts, a few more, taking lessons the whole time. Then I was in The Last Perfect Day, and it was a legitimate blockbuster, and everything changed. Suddenly I couldn't go anywhere without being recognized, like, anywhere in the developed world it seemed. People scream my name, red carpets are laid out, photo shoots, interviews, autographs, live chatrooms, script readings, auditions. It hasn't stopped since that movie. I try so hard and now it's like everybody wants me." I looked up at Nick for a second and then back down again. "But my first memory is always there. It's why I'll always be scared that none of this is real. How could it be real when my own parents didn't want me? It's all a trick, right?"

"Do you want it to be real?" he asked.

"Some of it."

"It's a shame we can't choose."

Nick propped himself up on his elbow, my head still resting on his arm, and leaned over me. His face was dim in the darkness with the stars and moon behind him, except for his eyes that were still visibly blue even in the low light. He was so close that I could feel the warm puffs of his breath on my skin.

"Harper, maybe you've been giving so much for so long you don't even realize it anymore, but you're about as close to perfect as it gets. It's not because you're so beautiful and it's not because you're so talented, although you are both of those things. It's because you care so much about the people around you. You can't fake that, and it's not a matter of how hard you *try* to care, it's just who *you* are, you can't help it. Just don't forget to care for yourself sometimes too. I think anybody who didn't want you in their life is crazy. They lost out on something special."

At that moment, of all the things in the world I wanted to be real, I wanted Nick to be real the most. It was hard to believe I was here, at the place I usually only came alone to, with somebody like him.

There was more to him than a sexy bad boy exterior, more than the muscle-bound villain I'd thought of when I first saw him. So much more. I brought my hand up along his strong back, to the rear of his neck, and gently stroked there with my fingers as I looked into his eyes.

Our lips could only have been a couple of inches apart. Under my hand, I could feel Nick shivering in anticipation or some kind of self-restraint that was barely holding up under the pressure. After pouring my heart out I felt like it was filling up with something else, something better, and a voice just kept repeating in my mind *kissmekissmekissme*.

"Kiss me," I said. And he did.

Nick closed the distance and I tilted my head, waiting until the last moment to shut my eyes as his lips touched mine. I pulled him harder against me, and his hand slid up my cheek to bury itself in my hair as we kissed even deeper.

Our lips parted for a moment with a wet sound and a quick pant from me, then found each other again. From behind my closed eyelids, Nick felt like a huge strong presence just above me. He was the source of that something that was filling up my heart, which was pounding as hard as it ever had in my whole life.

My job made me an expert in fake kisses, and this wasn't one of them. This was real, I was sure of it. I moved my hand to the bottom of his shirt and slid it underneath, feeling the hard curves of his abs, the line of one of his scars.

Our lips came apart again and I let out a shivery breath of excitement. Feeling his bare skin under my fingertips at last was magic. Real magic that made it feel like the sun was coming up and shining on me for the first time.

Then the hood of the car made a loud, metallic crumpling sound, and I felt it move under us as our weight finally seemed to put a dent in it. It startled me a little, but the effect it had on Nick couldn't have been more dramatic if a gunshot had suddenly gone off. He gasped as if in panic and pushed my hand away, leaping off the car and standing next to it, facing away from me as I scrambled to a sitting position. I looked around wildly for some kind of danger but saw none.

"What is…" I began.

"I'm sorry," he said.

"It's OK. We'll pop the hood and push it out from the other side, no harm no…"

"No." He turned around and moved his hand back and forth in his direction and mine. "This. I'm sorry about this. I can't. We need to go."

"What are you…"

But he was already walking back to the gate.

Chapter 12: Harper

You don't know the meaning of 'awkward' until there's a man between your legs who apparently really doesn't want to be there. I wasn't sure if Nick would want to continue training me in Brazilian Jiu Jitsu, but he did eventually confirm by replying to my messages.

Now Nick was in my 'guard', which meant that I was on my back, he was kneeling between my legs, and my legs were wrapped around his waist. It hurt to have him so near and yet so far.

Physically he was near, but mentally he seemed to have put up some walls and was doing his level best to maintain them. I tried to talk to him about the night at the lookout, to find out what I did wrong, but he avoided the questions with apologies and the training. It made me doubt everything I'd seen, heard, and felt that night, everything I'd felt since I met him. I couldn't have been *that* bad at kissing. I mean, nobody had ever complained before.

For me, it had been the most romantic few seconds of my life. I'd never been able to open up like that to anybody else. Despite my doubts, every fiber of my being was screaming out to feel that way again, to not let something like that slip through my fingers. If only Nick would let it happen.

"Again," he said.

I grabbed the right cuff of his jacket with my left hand, hooked my left leg over the top of his arm, and moved my right leg so that my shin was sideways against his belly, then hooked my right arm under his left knee, kicked out with my left leg, and pushed with my right leg. The combination of movements rolled us to my left and we ended up with him flat on his back and me crouching over him with one knee on his stomach.

"Good! Now, from here you could just punch me in the face mercilessly, which would look great, but look where your shin is, right on my bicep with my forearm trapped behind your knee. You're basically in position for a biceps slicer. It's brutal, but most people wouldn't know the kind of damage you're doing, so maybe not any good for your movie."

"Hmm," I said, my mind elsewhere.

Nick looked at the clock and then back to me. "Looks like we're out of time."

I sighed. "I guess so."

I stood and Nick rolled to the side, off the mats, and regained his feet near the wall. All I wanted to do was wrap my arms around him, rest my head against his chest, and feel him hug me back. I looked away before I just embraced him on impulse, afraid he'd push me away.

"I'm gonna get going, Harper," he said.

I turned back to him. "Can you wait until after I've changed? I need to talk to you."

"Harper... I can't do..."

"OK, just listen. I don't know what happened the other night, but it hurts. You understand that?"

"I don't want..."

"I know. You don't want me to be hurt, but I am. I poured my heart out to you, Nick. You think I tell that to everybody?"

"No, I…"

"I tell it to *nobody*. Who could I tell? I can't talk to my family, I can't make them feel like I'm ungrateful for everything they did. If I talked to somebody else, it would probably go straight to the gossip magazines. Do you know how it felt like to finally have somebody to talk to?"

Nick looked down at his hands, idly working at the knot on his belt. "Yes, I do," he said quietly.

"This isn't you, Nick. It would be too easy to pretend like you don't feel anything, a big tough ex-Marine, all tattoos and scars, who doesn't care about anything anymore. But I know you do."

It was almost too quick to spot, but when I said 'scars', I saw him flinch and then tug his rash vest down to make sure his stomach was completely covered. I furrowed my brow.

"I see *you* under there, Nick. I'd be crazy to not want you in my life, to paraphrase one of my favorite people."

Nick smiled unhappily, still looking down.

"But I don't want to be hurt. I can handle it if you don't want to be with me, I can even take things as slow as you need. I can't live with the idea that we didn't give it a chance if it's what we both wanted."

Nick raised his eyes to meet mine, the fear in them so out of place in a man his size, with his strength, with his background. I could understand that though. There's no training in existence to make you immune to the pain you risk when you give somebody your heart.

"So what's it gonna be?" I asked. "You wanna give us a shot?"

My words hung out there all alone for a few seconds and I thought he might just let them drop without an answer. He closed his eyes, a little longer than a blink, and then looked at me. I was sure my heart was doing a thousand beats per minute.

Nick bent down and wrapped both arms around my back, one just below my butt and the other at chest-level, before lifting me clear off the ground in a tight embrace. I returned it eagerly, having his arms around me felt just as good, hell, just as perfect as I thought it would.

His face was buried against my neck and I leaned my head on his as I wrapped my legs around him. We held each other so closely that, for a moment, it was hard to feel like we were two different people, but finally he pulled back.

"I don't know what the hell I'm doing, Harper, but I want you. I want you more than anything."

He leaned in and kissed me, hard, like the brakes had just been taken off, turning around and pushing me against the wall. By the time we broke our kiss, I was breathless from more than just the latest workout. I bit my bottom lip.

"I want you too… so much. But I've got to go. Appointments," I said, bordering on blowing off my schedule for the foreseeable future.

Nick nodded, slowly releasing his grip until I slid down the wall to my feet, his muscular weight still pressed against me. I pulled him down for another kiss, touching my tongue to his and then nuzzling against him.

"This Friday is the Fans Choice Awards. You wanna be my date?"

"I thought you were already going with that Lucas guy." I did my best to show my mild disgust with a single facial expression. "He can take a balloon with his picture on it, he'd prefer it that way. I said I want *you*."

"I don't have anything to wear. Unless this is suitable?" Nick pointed at his gi.

"Let me take care of that. I really gotta go, though." I squeezed out from between Nick and the wall and made it a few steps across the mat before bouncing back to him, giving him another kiss before pulling away again. I wanted to do cartwheels and backflips all the way to the changing room. This was happiness.

Chapter 13: Nick

The first time I was ever in a limo was on prom night. A bunch of us hired it and split the cost. I thought that was pretty classy at the time, but it was an absolute piece of crap compared to this one.

It smelled new, as if the company unwrapped a fresh one every time they received a booking. Secret compartments were everywhere, in some cases blended into the upholstery so cleverly that I felt like a super-spy when I pulled a panel off and discovered some champagne flutes.

First it picked me up from my apartment, where a woman had arrived with a make-up bag to help me get ready for the award show. If word ever got back to the guys in the corps about that, well, it just didn't bear thinking about.

She wouldn't take no for an answer or see my reasoning that I was just going to be sitting in the audience. She had a job to do. So be it.

I stepped out of the limo when it came to a stop in front of Harper's door and walked towards it, seeing it open before I closed the distance. Harper appeared there and drove all other thoughts out of my mind. Obviously she'd spent a fair bit of time with somebody fussing over her appearance too.

Harper rocked the natural look, and I'd seen her in a gi more often than anything else. It was easy to forget that she was a movie star sometimes, but this was not one of those times.

She wore a plain, not that anything could truthfully be called plain on her, red dress that hugged her feminine shape closely and dipped not-quite-scandalously-low at the front, revealing the enticing swells of her breasts. Her make-up was more pronounced than usual, but still subtle. Her lips were pink and glossy, a little fuller than usual, and so very kissable. Her eyes were accentuated with some eyeliner, and she had just a touch of extra color to her cheeks.

It looked like the most time had been spent on her hair, which spilled over her shoulders in waves and a few ringlets. She was perfection.

Close behind her, seeing her off, were her parents and brother. I shook hands with them all, having never properly met them before, and they all expressed their thanks about what I did for Harper that day. Her mother's smile was about as tight-lipped as any human could pull off, though.

Thankfully, Harper insisted on heading back to the limo pretty much straight away and we were sipping champagne within minutes.

"Something your mom isn't happy about?"

"Uh… well, she's the one that kinda spearheaded that whole idea about me going to this show with Lucas. She's… pissed, shall we say? But she'll get over it."

"Why would she organize your date?"

"Well, you know, she's my 'manager'," Harper scare-quoted the word with her fingers, "so every public appearance is a PR opportunity that's, like, in her realm."

"I guess I'm not good PR."

"Like I said, she'll get over it. Cheers!"

We clinked glasses and talked until we were nearly at the event center. My jaw dropped when I saw the crowd of people there. The flash of cameras was constant, spotlights searched for absolutely nothing in the sky, and we pulled up at the end of a long queue of limos, waiting our turn to get out at the start of the red carpet.

"Holy crap," I said.

"Yeah, it can get pretty crazy. This is a small one thankfully. Sometimes it's like walking a marathon. I don't wear heels to those ones."

"This is small?"

"One of the smallest."

"Damn."

"Once we get out of the car, we're pretty much not going to be able to talk until we get inside. I'll have to stop a lot of times for photos, and maybe an interview or two. Once we get inside it will be fine though. Stay close so I don't get lost, OK?"

"Yeah… I'll do that."

"And, um, can we keep 'us' on the down low for now? Like our little secret?"

My heart sank. "Why?"

Harper reached out and put her hand on mine. "Hey, it's not because I don't want to shout it from the rooftops. It's all just… new, you know? I just want to get to know it myself before we show it to the world. Trust me, they're *going* to find out eventually."

"OK. Fair enough. Uh… does your family know?"

"No. Like I said, just our little secret. For now. Just a little while, OK?"

I squeezed her hand. "OK. I understand."

When we arrived at the front of the queue, I exited the vehicle first and I'd never seen anything quite like it. It was pandemonium, the screams, the flash photography, the people everywhere. It was nuts.

Harper stepped out behind me, and there was no strobe light in the world that could possibly have flashed at that frequency. I squinted against the glare and turned back to offer my hand to her, which she took. The people behind the ropes, seemingly some mix of fans and photographers, lost their damn minds.

One of the security guys closed the door to the limo and tapped the roof a couple of times to signal for the driver to move on. Harper walked ahead a few steps, put a hand on one hip, and pivoted to each side a few times while smiling. People screamed like maniacs.

Moving on, I stayed close as she'd said I should. So she didn't get lost. Yeah right. With all those people so close, so loud and fanatical, it felt like a dangerous situation. I found myself naturally gravitating to her right hand side, putting myself between the crowd and her, on guard for anybody that might slip through the event security team.

This was her world though. Harper put her hand gently on my arm and spoke through her smile, somehow barely moving her lips as she moved ahead again. "Don't worry, it's always like this."

She stood in front of a wall covered in logos of the major studios along with, presumably, the sponsors of the show and struck her pose again. Both ahead of us and behind, as other limos dropped off more people, similar scenes unfolded.

"Harper! Over here!"

"Harper, look to your left!"

"Your *other* left! Big smile!"

I'd never seen so many faces I recognized on people I'd never met all in one place. From further along the red carpet, walking against the general flow, came another one. With a smile almost as wide as Harper's came a face I would have voted to put in the dictionary next to 'smug'. Lucas Collins.

The cheering from behind the lines took on an even more feverish pitch as he approached Harper and they gave each other a light hug before smiling out at the crowd for a few seconds. Lucas leaned in and whispered something in Harper's ear before gesturing towards the frontlines of the throng.

Harper nodded and put one arm around his neck as he dipped her backwards, their faces poised so close they were almost kissing. I clamped down on the green-eyed monster that suddenly thrashed around inside me. I'd seen the posters for Pandora Rising enough by now to know a recreation of the pose when I saw it, but it sucked to see that pretty boy get more intimate with her than I was allowed to in public.

Once they were upright again, Harper looked at me and I joined them. It did my heart good to see his smile falter as I towered over him and we shook hands.

Chapter 14: Nick

Harper was right, once we were inside it was a hell of a lot calmer. All kinds of people came to talk to her as we slowly made our way through the foyer and towards the huge room the event was taking place in.

A-list actors and actresses, directors and people who thought I should know them shook my hand and thanked me for what I did for Harper. My head was spinning.

Our seats were about a third of the way back from the front row, and Harper had to sit on the aisle because she was nominated in the category of 'best one-liner' for something she said in the Dark Fox movie.

The show was awesome. They had actor and comedian Bobby Jenson hosting the show, and several bands performed a song or two each between presentations of awards. I looked around the audience and could barely understand how I ended up sitting in this seat.

All around me were the most beautiful people the 'industry' had to offer. Actresses and models were everywhere. My eyes widened for a second when I spotted a woman I was sure was a porn star.

"What are you looking for?" Harper said quietly.

"I just had to check something."

"What?"

"I'm here with the most beautiful woman in the room," I whispered in her ear.

Harper blushed and fixed me with a smile that I thought would melt me down to nothing. I had to look down before I could no longer stop myself from kissing her.

It didn't help much. Her thigh peeked out from the slit in the side of the red dress. When I looked a little higher, due to our height difference, I was looking right down her cleavage. There was no escape from her all-encompassing sex appeal.

Then I was right back up to her smile, which had taken on a somewhat-knowing quality now.

"My eyes are up here," she said innocently, folding her arms across her front just enough to push her breasts together a little bit more.

"I…"

"Nerds quote them," announced Bobby Jenson from his podium, "they live on long after we've forgotten who said them, the writers don't get credit for them, it's time to find out who wins the award for the best one-liner! Presenting this award are the woman who was paid to be topless in The Wayfarer Terminus and the guy who got his junk out backstage for free, Melanie Barr and Henry Ruskin!"

The pair came out from behind some curtains and Henry Ruskin pointed at Bobby Jenson, lifting his mic up.

"You said you would pay. I want my underwear back. Anyway, the nominees for the best one-liners are…"

The lights dimmed, as they had for the previous categories where a video clip was applicable, and a few scenes were played as Henry and Melanie alternated in reading out the nominees. Harper was last and I recognized the scene immediately.

The bad guy was in his headquarters, moving forward with his plans for global domination, having recently witnessed what he thought was the death of Dark Fox. About to take over the television and radio signals around the world, he was just talking aloud to his second-in-command about what he should call himself. The Red God? The Godking?

The camera cuts to Harper, in the Dark Fox costume, looking down on them from the rafters with a baseball bat over her shoulder. Cut and bruised, but far from dead, she makes her own suggestion.

"How about 'The Bloody Pulp'?"

Then she jumped and the clip ended, to applause from the crowd. I knew that Dark Fox went on to kick some ass, but it wasn't my favorite scene from the movie. I'd seen it on 'movie night' back when I was still in the corps. Harper's character comes into some money around half-way through the movie and suddenly decides to replace the home-made costume she'd been using up until that point.

That short dressing-montage followed by the big reveal when she opened the door and strode out for the first time pretty much made our day. Amazingly, Sex Change Steve had put it more eloquently than anybody else when he said 'holy fucking shit'. That was the lesbian perspective when Dark Fox officially went off-the-scale sexy.

"And the winner is…" said Melanie, opening a golden envelope and showing it to Henry.

"Dark Fox, Harper Bayliss!" finished Henry.

The screen changed to show Harper in her seat, with my shoulder at the side of the image, looking surprised and happy. She leaned over and gave me a quick hug before standing and making her way to the stage to accept her award.

Henry and Melanie handed over the little trophy, and there was much kissing-of-cheeks before Harper gave a quick speech.

"Wow, thank you all! Um... Thanks to the fans for voting, of course. Thanks to my wonderful family, who support my career all the time, I couldn't do it without you. Thanks to the director, Ben Meyer, who ordered about fifty takes of that scene with a different line each time, and all the people who worked on the Dark Fox movie to make it great. And... thanks to Nick. Um... that's about it, thank you all, I'm gonna go backstage now and hope Henry doesn't get his junk out again."

"Sorry, Harper, I make them put it in all my contracts," said Henry, just before the theme music drowned him out and the three of them went back through the curtains.

*****

My hand pressed on Harper's bare skin and I reached around until my fingertips slid just under the material of her backless dress. With one hand on the back of my neck and the other on the car seat steadying herself, her Fans Choice award was forgotten somewhere on the floor as we kissed.

It wasn't until the limo stopped for a moment that I looked out of the window to see us driving into the underground car park of a hotel. Making out with a girl like Harper would distract anybody though.

"You're not going home tonight?" I asked.

Harper shook her head. Her eyes, only an inch from mine, gave me an obvious invitation to not go home either.

A violent war waged inside of me. On one side, the forces of fear and doubt sent chills up my spine. On the other, the utter *need* for her threatened to set me on fire. Harper nuzzled her nose against mine. Our lips brushed together and this battle, at least, was won. The war went on, though.

Harper wiped her lip gloss off me with her thumb before we stepped out of the limo, and I was tortured by the necessity of keeping my hands off her until the door to her room clicked shut behind us. She kicked off her shoes and pushed at my jacket until I shrugged it off and it landed on the floor.

I bent down to kiss her and Harper strained up on the tips of her toes to meet me. In the midst of our kiss, I scooped her up the same way I had in the gym and she wrapped her legs around me once more, one hand loosening my tie as we both got as much oxygen as we could through our noses.

Harper flung my tie backwards as I reached back to find her bare thigh, which was again being shown off to good effect by the high slit of the dress and exacerbated by the fact that her legs were around me.

Her skin was impossibly smooth, like some kind of supple glass, and my hand slid upwards easily, flirting with the lower extremities of her tight ass. I felt the top two buttons of my shirt undone before the voice from my nightmares spoke up in my mind.

She would vomit at the sight of you.

A pained gasp escaped my lips and I slowly let Harper down, her lithe body rubbing against the hard evidence of my lust for her until her feet touched the ground again. I gently grasped her shoulders and slowly moved her an arms-length away.

"I... Harper, I..."

I didn't know what to say, or how to say it. I wanted her, and the way she looked at me said she wanted me too, but that would all change if the undressing got far enough.

Harper and I couldn't work out in the long run. The thought of her perfect skin contrasted against my injuries was almost ludicrous. No. If we did this tonight, then that fiery spark of desire in her deep brown eyes would be snuffed out.

Maybe it was selfish of me, but I couldn't handle that. Not so soon. After everything I'd been through, was it too much to ask for just a little time with Harper's illusions intact? Just to let her look at me like that for a little while longer?

"Harper, can we..."

"Wait," she said.

She stepped backwards and looked over her shoulder, picking something up off the floor that turned out to be my tie. She held it out in front of her with two hands and then brought it up to her face, laying the material over her eyes and tying it in a knot behind her head. After a pause that I dared not defile with even the slightest sound of breath, she asked a question.

"What would you do with me if nobody could see?" Harper brought one finger to her lips in what might have been an expression of curiosity, but in all likelihood was just a hell of a sexy thing to do. It was a pretty damn good question too.

Chapter 15: Harper

For a few seconds, everything was silent. I half expected the next thing I heard to be the sound of the door opening and closing as Nick left. I pulled my finger away from my lips and wrung my hands together nervously as I waited for whatever would happen.

In the world of poker, I supposed this would be called going 'all-in'. I wanted Nick and he said he wanted me, but there was something that held him back. My best guess after our last encounter in the gym was some kind of self-consciousness about his scars.

I didn't care about them, but I could understand better than most regarding constant judgments about what you looked like. What would Nick do if he was free from those judgments for a while? Maybe for the first time since he received those scars?

Nick was still wearing his shoes and I heard him take first one step in my direction, and then another. The physical distance between us wasn't great, but it took an agonizingly long time before I sensed he was right in front of me again, close enough to touch if I reached out.

Perhaps the real distance that had to be crossed was a mental one, maybe that's what took so long. When I felt his hand on my cheek, touching me as gently as if he thought I might break into a million pieces, I felt like my guess might have been right on the money.

I leaned into his hand, feeling the warmth as my skin tingled in excitement. In my self-imposed darkness, I could hear Nick's breathing, which seemed to shudder with every beat of his heart, his own excitement being slowly let out of some cage.

Nick's hand stroked down my cheek and along my neck. I shivered, desperate to reach out to him, to feel for the remaining buttons on his shirt or rip it off if I couldn't find them.

More than that, I wanted him to walk the rest of that mental distance, to really be with me. So I held myself back, made my hands drop to my sides while I waited. He caressed along my shoulder and down my arm before I felt his other hand on me, thumb on my cheek and fingers curled around the back of my head, buried in my hair. I looked up at him, where I imagined his face was on the other side of my blindfold, and couldn't stop myself licking my lips in preparation for the kiss I fiercely hoped was coming.

I wasn't disappointed. The kiss came, starting slowly but quickly becoming deeper and deeper, and I felt his tongue gently touching mine until our lips finally parted. I rose up on the balls of my feet, unconsciously following him for a few inches before I felt my breasts brush against his torso.

Nick's hand moved from my arm to my hip, then curled around to my ass and pulled my whole body against him. Once more I felt that almost intimidating bulge in his pants as I lowered my heels to the floor again, pressing into my belly this time and making clear-thinking all the more difficult.

The excitement made it feel almost like I couldn't get enough oxygen in each time I inhaled. I was breathing so deeply that my breasts squashed against him every time they rose and fell. I was at my breaking point. I wanted him so bad.

I felt Nick's hands move to my shoulders and slip the straps of my dress off so they hung loose around my upper arms. After pressing myself against him even harder for a second, I pulled away to let him push my dress down far enough so that it slid to the floor, leaving me in just my lacy black G-string and my makeshift blindfold.

"Harper... you're the most beautiful woman I've ever been with," he said.

"So, be with me," I said.

Nick kissed me again and my nipples brushed against his shirt, sending an unexpected jolt of pleasure into my body. I broke off the kiss with a quiet gasp and felt Nick step forward, pressing against me so that I had to take a half-step back.

He brought my hand up to the next button on his shirt as I heard first one of his shoes kicked off and then the other. I began working at them as he steered me backwards in the direction of the bedroom. With him touching me all over my body and his kisses raining down, it was a quite the feat of coordination, but by the time the back of my knees hit the bed, I was able to push his shirt off.

I strained against him, my soft chest pressing on his hard body. I blindly sought out his lips again, already breathless but wanting more, and moved my hand from his shoulder, across his pectoral muscles, and then over his abs.

I had to break away from the kiss when I laid my hand on his manhood through his pants, feeling his size with certainty for the first time. An Amazonian warrior woman might look petite next to Nick, so I was definitely in the best kind of trouble.

Nick pushed me back and followed me down, moving with me as I shuffled further onto the bed. I reached for the button on his pants, but he gently made me lie flat with a hand on my upper chest. I arched my back, pushing my breast against his hand as his fingers trailed down towards my hip.

When he gripped the flimsy material of my underwear, I first pushed down with my feet to raise my ass off the mattress, then lifted both of my legs straight up with my toes pointed until he had removed my second-to-last article of clothing completely. His right hand curled around the upper thigh of my left leg and I bent it at the knee, draping it over his shoulder as he began to kiss my right calf.

Lower and lower he kissed, until my left leg slipped from his shoulder and I was utterly exposed before him, still without the power of sight due to the blindfold. He was taking his time, seeming like he was going to kiss every square inch of my skin before moving on.

It was delicious, squirmy torture, especially when he reached the back of my knee and the faint hint of stubble tickled at the same time as he kissed. Nobody had ever spent any time kissing there, and I was caught off guard by how good it felt.

I couldn't hold back a moan of pleasure when he finally stopped teasing my unexpected erogenous zone and continued up my inner thigh, getting closer and closer to my sex. I'd never felt anything between my legs like I was feeling now without having even been touched there yet.

Somewhere between an itch that had been begging to be scratched for weeks, an electric tingle, and a slippery mess, I was so ready for his touch that I almost cried when I felt his hot breath on my most private place. When he finally put me out of my misery, I was almost feral with lust.

Nick soon had my head thrashing from side to side, my fingers running through his hair as he did what no man had taken the time to do for me before. When my climax took over my body, I lost all coherence and had no idea what I might have been squealing.

I could barely get my words out when the heartbeat pounding in my ears came down to a level that I could hear myself over. I needed him inside me.

"Get a... condom, get... a condom," I panted.

Nick pulled away, and from under my blindfold I could hear him rushing through the removal of his pants and the crinkle of foil as he presumably retrieved a condom from his wallet. The anticipation was a torment until he finally climbed back on the bed and over me.

I reached down and wrapped my fingers around him, and he put his hands on the bed on either side of me, leaning forward to kiss my lips as I guided his length to my entrance. I let my head fall the last few inches on to the pillow and wrapped my arms around the back of his neck as he filled me up completely.

Nick, mercifully, started slowly, kissing my neck and sending chills all over my body. Soon, though, I was holding on for dear life as he let go completely and surrendered to his needs, unleashing God only knew how many months of pent up emotion, self-doubt, and denial.

His hand moved to my hair and firmly grabbed a sizable fistful, giving it an urgent tug that made me gasp in response, and then he held it, exposing my neck to him even more as if he was some vampire making me his prey. It was so much like the images that had flashed through my mind the first time I'd seen Nick and thought of him as a bad boy.

I had started this, pushed for this, and up until this point, I'd been somewhat in control. I felt the balance of power, the seat of control, shift from me to him as the feel of him inside me, the power of him holding me, put him in charge. I was just along for the ride, the sweet pleasure of the ride.

Nick's tie came loose, fell from my eyes, and I saw him naked for the first time. His body was a painful work of art, perfectly sculpted and then adorned with tattoos and crisscrossed with scars.

The faint red splash from the acid attack was barely noticeable and might even fade completely with time. All I could see was perfection though.

I curled my hand around the back of his neck and pulled his forehead against mine, bringing his eyes so close that they were all I could see. The fire of my second orgasm took over and I struggled against the urge to squeeze my own eyes shut, just wanting to swim in his clear blue forever.

Nick looked back at me. Even in the haze of his lust he knew that I could see him, and it didn't hurt anymore. It didn't hurt him at all.

Chapter 16: Nick

Consciousness crept up on me slowly as I awoke from the kind of sleep normally reserved for recovery after a full day of marching. By the time Harper and I finished the previous night, we were as exhausted as we'd ever been after a BJJ session.

The first thing I noticed, before I'd even opened my eyes, was the faint smell of vanilla. I was on my side and Harper was beside me, facing the other way, the entire length of her perfect body pressed against mine. The vanilla scent was coming from her hair. I took a deep breath through my nose and opened my eyelids just a crack. I could just make out the side of her face as she slept peacefully.

I licked my lips and got the idea, not as obvious as a real *flavor*, but just the idea of strawberries, and I thought of Harper's lip gloss. She had kissed me, she had *seen* me. It was still a concept that warranted skepticism. Harper. And me.

Under the covers, my arm was draped over her and she had fallen asleep hugging it between her breasts, her fingers interlaced with mine. Everything was silent except for the faint sound of Harper breathing.

The whole room was quiet. Maybe the whole world had stopped so I could stay in this moment forever. That would be fine by me. If there was a heaven, this was what it would be like.

It felt like life had, recently, been nothing but unbearable heat and choking dust. I couldn't breathe, everything was so *hard*, so *sharp*, and there was nowhere to rest. I'd only been waking up each day out of habit. There was no other reason for it.

Then Harper came along. And she was cool. She was fresh air. She was soft. I took another deep breath. She smelled *good*. She felt like home.

Home. That used to mean something else besides Harper. Some*one* else. A long time ago I'd given my heart to Christie and assumed that it would always belong to her. We'd promised each other forever.

For the first time in months, I let myself think about Christie. The memories came to me like a series of pictures on the wall of a decrepit old house. They were dirty and cracked but, when I wiped the dust off, the colors underneath were still beautiful.

God it hurt, the way she looked at me in those memories. She trusted me, but she didn't know that our forever was going to be a lot shorter than some others. Neither did I. A tear fell out of the corner of my eye and landed somewhere in Harper's hair.

If I was really going to do this, if I was going to 'give us a shot' with Harper, I had to come clean about Christie. Harper had to know that I wore the worst scars on the inside.

I paused, trying to memorize every single little detail of this momentary heaven I'd woken up to this morning in case I never woke up to anything like it again. With a kind of internal sigh, I carefully disentangled my arm from Harper and eased myself backwards and out of the bed.

In her slumber, Harper sighed. It was a sound slightly reminiscent of some of those sexy little noises she had made last night, though much more subdued.

I found my underwear and pulled them on as Harper rolled on to her back and pulled the covers up over her shoulders. She let out a sleepy little growl of annoyance without opening her eyes or even her mouth, not quite awake yet but definitely stirring.

My wallet was on the bedside table where I'd hurriedly dropped it after retrieving a condom I'd first thought would probably expire before I bothered using it.

There was something else in there though, a picture I had tucked in behind all the bank cards and hadn't taken out since I returned home from the Marine Corps to find out that everything I cared about the most was gone.

I picked the wallet up and sat back down on the bed, rifling through the cards until I got to the back and ran my finger along the somewhat tattered edge of the photograph. Harper took a deep breath behind me, and I could sense her stretching out as the mattress and covers shifted with her movements.

"Morning," she said.

"Morning," I replied in a low voice.

"Everything OK?"

Harper sat up, sheet wrapped around her chest, and peered around the side of my arm to see my wallet in my hands.

"No charge," she said.

"Harper, we have to talk. I need to tell you something."

"What is it?" she said quietly, pulling the sheet more tightly around herself.

I tugged the photo out and averted my eyes as I passed it over my shoulder to Harper. I knew what it looked like, I didn't need to see it. I still couldn't look at it anyway.

It was taken shortly before I shipped out for the first time, Christie and me kissing, with eyes squeezed shut and fish-lips sticking out from our faces, as she held the camera out at arms-length. It was a miracle we were in frame at all, let alone perfectly centered and caught in a moment so silly and sweet that the very thought of it still ripped me apart.

"Who's this?"

"My girlfriend."

"What?" Harper's question was like a judge's gavel.

"My... my..."

"Are you *cheating* on her with me?"

I'd never said it before. To say it aloud would be admitting it was true, and I'd not yet been able to face up to that reality. For Harper, though, I had to. I couldn't give Harper my heart until I'd taken it back from Christie. Until I'd let Christie go.

"My... ex... girlfriend. Ex."

"Why do you still have her picture in your wallet?"

"She's not... she... she's... she died. And it's my fault. She saved my life and I couldn't save hers."

Harper brought one hand across her mouth as she looked back and forth between the photo and me. I could see tears welling up in her eyes as that part of her that cared so much about people took over.

"W-what's her name?"

"Her name is Christie. Well, Christabelle, really."

"That's a pretty name. She's really beautiful too."

Harper handed me the picture back and I held it between the fingers and thumbs of both hands, still not quite able to view it directly. The slightly faded colors floated in the lower periphery of my vision, daring me to look.

"Yeah. A name like that, you know her mom wanted to dress her up as a little princess ever since she found out she was having a girl," I said.

"Yup."

"Must have really pissed her off that her little girl just wanted to be called 'Chris'. When I tell you she was a tomboy, you better believe it. Oh, man."

"You knew her when you were kids?"

"Oh yeah, we knew each other since we were about five years old. But, you know, kids are like boys over here and girls over there. We didn't really have all that much to do with each other until we were eight. That's when we were… uh… properly introduced."

"How?" Harper shuffled forward and leaned against me, her head resting on my upper arm.

"In the only way an eight-year-old boy knows how to introduce himself. I put glue in her hair, of course."

Harper tentatively smiled. "You Casanova."

"Yeah, but remember how I said she was a tomboy?"

"Uh oh."

"Whoa. She turned around and kicked me in the balls *so hard* that I swear I was lifted a good foot off the ground."

I could see Harper was smiling even though I could feel the wetness against my arm. "Girl power," she said.

"To this day, I swear my voice is a full octave higher than it otherwise would have been. The agony. So Christie's mom eventually gets to hear about this whole incident in the principal's office, as do my parents. I thought my punishment was bad enough. I had to make her an apology card, which I was supposed to give to her the next day. I thought *my* parents were strict, but you should have seen Christie."

"What do you mean?"

"Well, I guess this was the straw that broke her mom's back. After years of dainty little dresses getting ripped and muddy, dolls set on fire and who knows what else, she snapped. She could have just cut out the bit of hair with the glue in it, but she didn't."

"She left it in?"

"No. She shaved it right down the middle and made her come to school for the rest of the week like that. My apology card was… not well received. It went straight in the trash as soon as the teacher wasn't looking. Her mom eventually made Christie sign up sponsors and then shave her whole head for cancer research, but that's how years of enmity between us began."

"It's not quite Romeo and Juliet," said Harper.

"No. It took a long time. I hated her as much as she hated me until we started high school. I don't know what magic was worked in those summer holidays, but when she came to school, Chris was gone and then she was Christie."

"Did you ask her out?"

"Like everybody else, yeah. I won't tell you *exactly* what she said, but it wasn't 'yes'."

Harper stroked my arm with her hand, shuffling even closer.

"We kinda went our separate ways for a while. I got my growth spurt and started getting into a few fights here and there. Fell in with the wrong crowd too. Every few months or a year, I'd ask her out again, but she always shot me down."

I looked down at Harper, then finally at the happy moment caught in the picture. The sound of her voice from the past hit me like a ton of bricks. What had she said when she held out the camera? *Kissyface!* My breath hitched and I looked away again. Harper's other hand came up to my shoulder, giving it a little rub.

"I know what people see when they look at me, Harper. Some violent criminal, probably on drugs, probably going to get shot for no good reason soon. That's just what I was turning into when Christie finally said yes." I closed my eyes and pictured her there, arms crossed and laying down the law for me. It was so vivid, I could almost reach out and touch her.

"We went on a date. I laid on as much charm as I had and we, somehow, hit it off. I was hooked on her right from the start and I think she was hooked on me too, but she wouldn't date me anymore until I promised her something."

"Promised what?" Harper asked.

"She said my friends were a bunch of assholes. She wasn't going to date some drugged-out douche getting into brawls on the weekends and stealing things. If I wanted to be with her, I had to make some pretty big changes, leave a lot of stuff behind."

"But you did."

"She was... worth it," I said. "Nobody was ever proud of me the way Christie was proud of me. The guys I used to hang out with, a couple months later they went to the next town over and broke into somebody's house. That somebody shot one of them. Boom. Dead. If it wasn't for Christie, I might have been there. You know how I said I joined the Marines because of my dad?"

"Yeah."

I shook my head and tapped the photo. "This. This here is the real reason. I got this idea in my head that I had to go out *there* to make sure Christie was always safe, I had to do my bit to make sure the best thing in the world was defended. My dad had always wanted me to do something like that, so it seemed like a good idea."

My throat closed up on me and I rested my forehead on one hand to force the air in and out, feeling like somebody was scrubbing my insides with a piece of steel wool. My stomach cramped and I winced. Harper rubbed my back, a wordless supportive presence.

"What happened?" she asked.

"The last time I had leave, before I got captured, I remember Christie there at the airport telling me not to go, to just be one day late. We'd go somewhere so we could have one day all to ourselves. Just one day. I told her I couldn't, I had to be where I was told to be. I had orders. I'd give anything to have told her yes instead."

"Then you got captured."

"Yeah, but I went missing first. They found... pieces... of some of the guys I was with, others were just all shot up. They had no idea where I was, or if there was anything left of me to find. Well, my dad had passed away after I'd been in the corps for a few years, my mom just after I graduated high school. By then I had Christie as my contact in case of emergency. They told her I was missing and presumed dead."

"Oh no," said Harper, the last word drawn into a kind of horrified groan. "I don't know what..."

"Christie didn't take it too well, so she went back to her parents' place and locked herself in her old room for days. She went out one night for a walk. In Warfields. The little town where nothing ever happens. Well…"

"What happened? Nick?"

"Somebody attacked her. There aren't a lot of details. All they ever found was blood on the sidewalk, a *lot* of blood, and some drag marks. They searched for months but, with that much blood, they had to conclude, on the balance of probabilities, that she had been… killed. She was out there because of me."

"Nick, it's not your fault. You know that, right?"

"The same way you know your parents didn't leave you in that group home because you spilled too much juice? Like you said, it sticks with you."

Harper looked down for a moment and nodded. "Yes, it does."

"So, I was rescued, I recovered pretty quickly, I was back on my feet soon. I got all these… these scars. The guy wanted to send me back home dead, so disfigured that I'd need a closed-casket ceremony. He didn't have enough time to finish his work, but when I woke up in the medical tent I thought, 'Ha! You can't kill me, you fuckers'. Then in a hospital in Germany I was thinking to myself, 'Why have I not heard from Christie? What did they tell her?' It wasn't until I got home that I found out what happened and I realize that they *did* kill me. I didn't manage to protect anything."

"I'm so sorry, Nick," said Harper.

"Me too. I managed to get discharged based on what happened while I was captured, said I couldn't go on, my head wasn't in the right place. There was nothing left for me in Warfields either. All the friends I had there were Christie's friends, or mutual friends. They looked at me the way everybody else has since then, with a bit of blame thrown in for good measure. I sold the old family home and after Christie was declared legally... dead, I've been just wandering around. I didn't know what I was doing, no plans, just taking odd jobs here and there to keep busy, to stop myself from eating into the savings too quickly."

I tucked the photo back into my wallet, in its spot behind the cards, and put my wallet back on the bedside table before turning to Harper, scared about what I'd find written there on her face.

"I couldn't save her," I said. "I'm no hero."

"You saved *me*."

Harper grabbed the sheet, which was being held up between our bodies, and wrapped it around my front, pulling me back into the bed and leaning over me. I fought back the instinct to push her hand away when she rested it on my bare chest, right on some of the worst scars, but there was no revulsion on her face. She still looked at me the same as she had the previous night.

"You were right there when I needed you," she said, nuzzling herself down with my arm around her and her head resting in my armpit. "I *needed* you."

"I love you, Harper," I said, and let the words stand out there by themselves. It didn't matter if she felt the same, what I'd said was the truth either way. I felt like a whole person again.

Chapter 17: Harper

After the Fans Choice Awards, I was out of town for almost a week, most of the time spent at a comic book convention where I was part of a panel because of having been in the Dark Fox movie. After a hell of a lot of problems in post-production, it had eventually made it to theatres almost a year after filming actually finished, and this was the first convention since the release.

The big news for fans was the official announcement that 'Dark Fox 2: The Fall' was going to start filming soon, with a release date next summer. It was humbling to see how much of a following the character had, especially considering all the amazing competition in the genre. People went crazy when the short clip revealing the title played on the screen above us.

It was strange being on the road with my mom and Orson again, away from home. I didn't like to be away from Nick after such an incredible night and a revealing morning either.

Him saying he loved me was unexpected. If I counted social media, then I probably received anywhere between five and ten thousand declarations of love a day, but I had a feeling that with Nick, it wasn't something he said lightly.

Neither did I, which is why I didn't say it back to him. Not because I didn't feel very strongly for him, but because I'd never been in love before. I needed some time to think about exactly what this churning volcano of joy I felt inside really was. He had the advantage of having been in love once already, maybe that was why he could say it.

On the third day into my trip, I sent him a text and didn't get a reply all day. I couldn't stop myself from worrying. Nick was a big boy, but what if something had happened to him?

Only last year, Nick had said goodbye to Christie before getting on a plane and then he never saw her again. Things happen.

The thought that I'd never look into his eyes again, never have those strong arms around me and feel like I was as safe as if I was in Fort Knox, never have him to talk to again, was almost too much to bear. The possibility that I could lose the one person I'd found in the world that I trusted with my deepest secrets, and who trusted me the same way in return, was horrific.

It wasn't easy, but I made myself stay calm. I didn't want him to look at his phone and see a hundred and thirty seven texts, fifty missed calls, and a couple dozen voicemails, but it made me realize that there was nothing, and had never been anything, in my life that made me happier than being with Nick. I loved him, for sure.

He eventually called back and said he'd left his phone at home that day before working a security shift for Jeremy Holt. Hypothetical crisis averted.

I didn't tell him I loved him over the phone. It seemed like something that should be done in person. In my mind I went over different scenarios, envisioning grand romantic scenes inspired by some of my favorite movies, where everything culminated into the perfect moment for me to tell him how I felt.

The daydreams were so enthralling that as I sat on the panel at the convention, I flat out missed a question directed at me, to the amusement of everybody present. That night, going against my better judgment and long-standing policy, I looked up a video of the event in question and watched myself sitting there with my face all smooshed up by my cheek resting on my hand as I stared off into the distance with a ditzy smile on my lips.

The comments below speculated that I was on drugs. Some of them talked about my date to the Fans Choice Awards. It seemed like the time for my relationship to be my little secret was already almost over.

*****

As soon as I was back in town, I grabbed some things and went to Nick's apartment for the night. It was small and tidy, furnished by whoever his landlord was and obviously furnished from stores at the cheaper end of the scale. It had everything he needed though, and with him there it had everything I needed too.

After being away from each other for a week, I couldn't keep my hands off him and it seemed the feeling was mutual. From the moment he lifted me up and set me down on the kitchen counter, moving between my legs to get good and close, to the moment we fell asleep, we were never out of physical contact for very long.

The reunion was passionate, heavy, but the sex this time was slower and more deliberate than in the hotel after the award show. I'd never felt so happy that I could cry before, but this was mighty close and it pained me to have to keep appointments the next morning.

Thankfully we had a BJJ session scheduled for that afternoon. Of all the hours of training he'd given me this was, hands down, the least productive. Every time he was close enough, we ended up kissing, making out until we remembered what we were supposed to be doing and I had to learn the technique again from the beginning.

I was supposed to be choking him out with his own collar, but instead I pulled him close and whispered in his ear.

"I love you."

It was nothing like the movies. There were no fireworks, no popping of a champagne bottle, but if I didn't say it, I was going to explode. Nick smiled and kissed me again, about as fearful of my ability to choke him unconscious as he should have been.

Time flies when you're having fun, and this was no exception. The training session was over almost before it started. I knelt by my sports bag and pulled out my bottle of water, much less desperate for it than at the end of any other session.

Nick leaned against the wall. "What're your plans for the rest of the day?"

"Well, I'm glad you asked. I've got something called 'free time'... did I say that right? Freeeee tiiiiime?"

"Close enough. What are you going to do?" he asked with the tiniest of smirks.

"Thought I'd go to the beach. Thought *we* might go to the beach,"

The corner of Nick's mouth fell, and the smirk disappeared as he looked down at his hands and began untying his belt to keep them busy.

"I don't really go to beaches. Besides, can you go to a beach without being mobbed?"

"If I can get to the beach without bringing a crowd, then the people already there usually leave me alone. Some people might ask for a photo or autograph, but if you're there, I'll be fine. You sure you can't come?" I pulled my secret weapon out of my sports bag. "Because I just bought this new bikini and I *really* wanted to show you what it looks like on me. I might need some help with my sunscreen too…"

*****

With our smoothies to-go, I acted as navigator and Nick drove us to Manhattan Beach. It was a bit more inconvenient to get to, but also much less crowded as a result. I'd put my bikini on under my t-shirt and jeans back at the gym and loved the puppy-dog eyes Nick gave me when we threw down our towels and I did the big reveal.

Nick wore the shorts from his pre-session workout, plus his rash vest. He ran down to the water, diving in and coming straight back out while I was still setting up our little spot and putting my clothes away. He tried to look nonchalant while I was putting the sunscreen on my chest, but I guessed he had even less acting experience than I had when I applied for my first role. "Here. Do my back, would ya?" I held out the bottle. It was sweet torture for me to have his hands on my bare skin and not to go further. I wanted to turn around and straddle him right then and there, but this was a family-friendly beach.

In addition to that, there was the whole 'our little secret' thing. It was a wonderful trip to the beach. We talked, splashed around, played with a Frisbee, but time and again we found ourselves closer than friendship-distance and we'd go quiet.

I could see how much he wanted to reach out and touch me, I was sure the expression on my face was exactly the same. It was hard to remember why I wanted to keep it a secret. Because it was new? Because I wanted to get to know it myself first? Hadn't I figured that out while I was away?

"You're getting burned," I said. "Did you put sunscreen on?"

"Ah... no. I forgot."

I rummaged around in my bag until I found it and handed the bottle over. Nick took it and applied it over his face and the exposed parts of his body as we sat and looked out over the water, then handed it back.

"Excuse me..." came a sheepish voice.

I looked to my right and saw a little girl half-hidden behind the leg of her mother, clutching a pink lunchbox. She was adorable, and I couldn't help but smile.

"Hello?" I said.

The girl looked up at her mom and then mustered up all the courage she had. "My mommy says you're Princess Sundancer all grown up and if I ask really *really* REALLY nice, you might sign my lunchbox. Are you really?"

"Sorry to bother you," said the woman.

"It's OK," I said, then looked back down at the girl. "What's your name?"

"Harper," said the girl.

"That's a nice name," I said, with a chuckle and a wink at her mom. "Your mommy is right, Harper, I'll sign it if you, very quietly, just tell me what the magic word is."

"Kazoosh!" said the girl, nowhere near quietly, and held out the lunchbox along with a felt pen.

"That's right!" I laughed and put my mark on the lid before handing them both back.

"I thought you were great in Those Lost Ones, that's my favorite of yours," said the woman.

"Thank you so much!" I said.

"Mommy, what?"

"Never mind, sweetie, what do you say?" she said.

The girl looked unsatisfied with the answer but was distracted enough by the new writing on her Princess Sundancer lunchbox that she didn't pursue it any further.

"Thank you!" she said.

"You're welcome."

The two of them left with a wave and I turned back to Nick, spotting a white smudge of sunscreen he hadn't rubbed in properly on the back of his neck. Behind him, a fairly long way away and holding a camera with a huge lens, was a paparazzo taking photos, as they did. Well, this would set the rumor mill going, that was for sure.

"You're really good with people," said Nick.

"That kid was so sweet. Hey..."

I brought myself up to my knees behind Nick and slowly rubbed the sunscreen in.

"There's a photographer over there. Want to make his day?"

Nick glanced over. "It's not a topless beach, Harper."

I slapped his shoulder playfully. "Not that. This."

Pulling Nick backwards, I shifted to the side to get out of the way and then leaned over him, tucking my hair behind my ears as I got closer.

"You sure?" he said.

"Time to shout it from the rooftops. I want everybody to know how lucky I am."

We kissed and although he was too far away for me to be certain, I thought the photographer's eyes probably turned into dollar signs as he clicked away.

Chapter 18: Harper

I heard the alarm go off and reached out in every direction before I even opened my eyes, searching for Nick, before I woke up enough to remember that I was at home alone in my own bed. I picked up my phone and turned the alarm off with a sigh. No rest for the wicked *or* me.

With eyes still half-closed, I sleepily shuffled across my room to my drawers and found what I needed to go for a run, getting dressed on auto-pilot. My reflection in the mirror elicited a mock-scream and I brushed my hair until I could manage to gather it all into a ponytail and went downstairs.

In the kitchen, my dad was just putting his breakfast dishes in the dishwasher. You had to get up pretty early in the morning to be up earlier in the morning than him.

"Morning Dad, still not retired?"

"Apparently not, honey. Morning."

My income would have the whole family more than covered if push came to shove for some reason, but unlike Orson and my mom, Dad didn't want to get involved in the movie business. Even after The Last Perfect Day, when seven-figure contracts started being bandied about, he kept plugging his way up the corporate ladder in his own job.

I poured myself some juice and had a look out the window, hoping for good running weather. My dad put on his suit jacket, and gave me a kiss on the cheek.

"Fair warning, Harp, your mom's on the warpath this morning."

"Ugh. About what?"

"Take a guess."

"Nick?"

"And all that entails," he said.

"He's… he's a good person, Dad. The best person. I'm in… I love him. You know?"

"I'm not telling you what to do, Harper, you're twenty years old. For what it's worth, I've never seen you so happy. Your mom's sacrificed a lot for your career though, and things have worked out pretty well on that front. So pick your battles wisely."

"OK. Thanks. Have a good day."

My juice was barely finished when I heard footsteps coming down the stairs and braced myself for an onslaught. My jaw clenched, waiting for the inevitable.

"Morning, Harp!" said Orson.

I let out a puff of air, unwinding for the moment, and turned around. Orson was wearing his running gear too, looking ready to go.

"Morning. Where's Mom?"

"I think I heard the shower going, why?"

"Nothing. You ready?"

"Can I at least get some toast first?"

"I really want to get an early start on the Dark Fox 2 lines, can we just go?"

Orson held up his hands. "Fine, fine."

It was a good time of day to be running, light enough to see where you were going but the air was not yet heated up enough to make things uncomfortable. Orson and I ran most mornings when we were both home, and going for a run sometimes seemed like the closest thing I got to free time.

Although Orson always came with me for security purposes, it wasn't a social thing. Sometimes I listened to lessons from a dialect coach on my iPod if I was involved in a role that required a particular accent. Once, I had listened to an audiobook version of a movie-adaptation I was cast in.

Usually it was just music, but the most important thing about going for a run was the chance to be alone with my thoughts. When I really wanted to think, I had a track on my iPod that was just "Rain on a tin roof with thunder" for two entire hours. That's what I played this morning.

When I was in a rage or my heart was broken like when my first real boyfriend cheated on me, when my mind left the building, I went on a run to find it, and it almost always worked. I kind of depended on them sometimes.

We always ran the same route. That made it easier for me to think about things other than where we were going. Left out of our gate and all the way along our road and into the park, clockwise around the little man-made lake, out of the park and then up the hill and down the other side before looping back around and arriving back on our street at the opposite end.

By the time we returned, I hadn't had the 'eureka' moment I was hoping for and when we stepped inside to the smell of coffee, I knew our mom was waiting for me. Sure enough, she was at the kitchen table with her trusty tablet PC, reading something.

"Harper, we need to talk," she said.

"Mom…"

"This… this thing, whatever you're doing with this Nick boy, has got to stop. They found an old friend of his who's talking about all the drugs they used to do in school, another anonymous associate who says he was discharged from the Marines because he lost his mind about something. You only have to look at him to…"

"To *what*, Mom? Have you forgotten what he *did* for me?"

"Harper, I know you're grateful, but you're taking your gratitude too far…"

I saw red, absolute mind-numbing rage. Could she, the woman who raised me, really be implying what I thought she was implying?

"You think I'd… you think I'd have *sex* with him because I'm grateful?"

"Oh no, Harper, don't tell me it's gone that far…"

"You're right, it's none of your business!" I yelled. Orson was frozen in place behind the breakfast bar, hand in the bag of bread as he stared at us with an open mouth. My mom stood and approached me, as calm and assured of herself as if she was talking to a child having a tantrum.

"What's gotten into you?" she asked. "This isn't like you at all! I haven't forgotten what Nick did, but that doesn't mean he's right for you. We've worked for so long, for most of your *life*, so that you can live the dream. You've got this wholesome image because you are a wholesome girl. Everybody wants to work with you because you're a professional. Since you met him he's been damaging that image and your mind has been all over the place. People have noticed."

"I honestly don't care," I said.

My mom couldn't have looked more shocked if I had shot her in the foot. She shook her head as if recovering from a daze and blinked like she had something in her eyes.

"Harper, has he got you on drugs?"

"Mom, don't be stupid. *He* isn't even on drugs himself."

"As far as you know. This behavior is so disappointing. There's more than just your job on the line, this is a family business now, you know. Is this how you repay me after everything I've done? How could you do that to me? Imagine if I'd never come along."

I hadn't dared to cross my mom's path too many times in my life, but if it ever got too far, she always managed to remind me, either directly or indirectly, that she had rescued me from the group home. The loneliness and dull terror I'd felt on a day-to-day basis in that place was so dark compared to the happy home this family had given me. It always took all the wind out of my sails.

The anger drained away, deflating me and leaving me feeling about as big as a mouse. Oh yes, I remembered all too well what she saved me from, the love she'd shown me, the home she'd given me.

"I'm sorry, Mom," I forced out.

"Attagirl. We all make mistakes. You just let him down nicely, you never know how badly a man like him might take it, and we can get on with life. You'll be able to concentrate on the audition for Great Expectations on Monday. No doubt you'll get the part, and then shooting for Dark Fox Two starts Thursday…"

"I'm *sorry*, Mom… but I'm *not* breaking up with Nick. It's not your choice to make. I love him. And I'm not doing Great Expectations. I'm sorry… I love you too." I left the kitchen at an almost-run all the way back to my room, feeling about as scared as if I'd poked a hornet's nest with a stick and ashamed for being so scared at the same time. The last thing I wanted was for her, Dad, and Orson to stop loving me, to disown me and make me an orphan again at the age of twenty. I didn't want to be alone like that ever again. Never. I'd been abandoned by one set of parents before and I didn't think I could handle it another time. But I couldn't give up Nick either. I thought about burying myself in a big Nick-hug, and it helped me fight away the tears.

Chapter 19: Nick

With the last of the dishes put away, I did one last inspection of my apartment. It was sparsely furnished, so it didn't take very long. Even now it was hard to imagine a girl like Harper in such plain surroundings, but she'd been here before and her text confirmed she'd be here again any moment.

My phone had never seen so much action. People I hadn't heard from in years were calling and texting, sending messages from the sublime to the ridiculous, congratulatory and crass. It was a strange feeling to be put under the spotlight like that.

The intercom buzzed and after a 'Hello?' and 'It's me', I pressed the button to let her in the building and waited by the door. I drummed my fingers on my thigh, feeling this humming excitement in my stomach like I used to feel on Christmas morning when I was a kid. For the first time since I found out about Christie, there was something to look forward to. Not just some pie-in-the-sky one day I might win the lottery kind of dreams. Something even better, closer, sooner, more tangible. She was probably walking down the hallway right now.

The knock on the door confirmed that assumption and I opened it right away. Harper stepped through and threw her overnight bag on the floor unceremoniously before wrapping her arms around me and burying her face against my chest.

She looked tired, not like after we'd trained together, but simply worn down by something. When I hugged her back I could feel her pressing as close as possible, as if she wanted to melt into me, and she relaxed her legs a bit, letting me bear some of her weight.

I flicked the door closed behind her and held her for a while, resting my cheek on the top of her head. Tired or not, she still smelled like heaven with a faint sense of vanilla. Finally, she stood on her own power again. "You look like you could do with a glass of wine," I said.

"Oh yeah. Yes please."

Harper picked up her bag and put it in my room before heading to the couch, sitting down, and kicking her feet up sideways to lie down. I could see her dark hair flowing over the armrest from my vantage point as I took the wine out of the fridge and popped the cork, which came out with a massive bang and ended up putting a tiny dent in the ceiling.

"Whoa. Was that a bottle of wine or a gun?" she asked.

"I need higher ceilings," I said as I poured. "You look tired. Busy day?"

"Yeah, Dark Fox Two starts filming late next week and I've been practicing my lines with Orson for most of the day."

Harper shuffled back against the armrest and sat a bit more upright when I brought the wine over and handed her one. I sat down and pulled her legs over my lap like a little blanket before clinking glasses.

"Cheers. You find that tougher than the interviews and all the promo stuff?"

"Nah, it's not that. I'm having a tough time with my mom at the moment."

"About what?"

Harper looked at me for a second and then looked down at her wine before taking a sip. She licked her lips and let out a little sigh.

"I've been thinking about it all day. It's not even this latest problem that is the *big* issue. You know how the Bayliss family adopted me?"

"Yeah," I said.

"I think one thing I've been scared of this whole time, my whole life since then, was that something would happen and I'd lose my family. Then it would be just like I was in the group home again. I mean… it'd be different, but it would still feel the same. You know?"

"Sure, I can see that. But odds are nothing is going to happen to them, Harper."

"That's the thing, though. Something *did* happen. That's what I've been thinking about today. Ever since The Last Perfect Day hit it big and things got crazy, I lost my mom and gained a manager. And that sucks. All she wants to do is run my life, nothing's more important to her than my career."

"Hmm. What's the latest battle you're having with her?"

"Uh… well, I'm supposed to be going in to read for another movie-adaptation of Great Expectations next week, but I don't want to do it. She doesn't want me to be typecast with doing too many action and adventure style movies."

"I hate Great Expectations," I said.

"What? The last movie, the book, or what?"

"Everything that it is, everything that it stands for."

Harper gave me a sideways look and raised her eyebrow. "That's a pretty… strong stance to take, isn't it?"

"No. I had a bad experience with the book when I was a kid."

The movie star on my couch snorted out a laugh and then covered her mouth with her hand, a little sparkle seeming to light up her eyes. When she took it away, I could see she was smiling.

"Did the book... do *bad* things to you, Nick?"

"I accidentally read it when I was about ten years old." Harper laughed again. "Accidentally? How do you accidentally read a whole book? Oh, wait, wait, is that some macho thing? Like you can't admit that you read a book like that so you call it an accident? Like after the award show how your clothes mysteriously disappeared and you accidentally fell on me a few hundred times?"

"First of all, it was a thousand times at least, and second of all, I swear I didn't mean to read this book." Harper was shaking with laughter now and let out a little squeal when some of her wine slopped out of her glass and landed on her shirt. She reached out and grabbed on to my arm as if to steady herself.

"You gotta... you gotta tell me how," she stammered out between slowly dwindling chuckles.

"OK. So there I was, in school, minding my own business, and one of the things they made us do for a couple of hours a week was what they called Silent Sustained Reading. SSR for short. Did you have that?"

"I was home-schooled starting when I was about nine years old."

"Oh. Well, it was just teacher code for 'shut up for ten seconds so I can think about my life choices, please' but it forced us to read at least. So our classroom had a bunch of books in the corner and I was a bit slow choosing, and all the good ones were gone. I was flicking through them trying to find something, all the while being told in no uncertain terms that if I wasn't back at my desk by the count of three, I was in big trouble. That's when I saw it."

"The light at the end of the tunnel..."

"This plain green book with white letters, sticking spine-out on the shelf. It had an interesting title, so I grabbed it and ran back. It started out slow, but I thought I could live with that, like, sure, a bit of background information on the main characters might make it a better story, more exciting when they're out shooting lions or exploring old ruins or whatever."

"Lions? What the..." Harper's shoulders started shaking with the giggles again.

"I should have just put the book back and chosen a new one for the next SSR hour, but I thought it would get better. By the time I looked at how many pages were left and I knew that I was living in a house of lies, it was too late. I was going to finish the book or die trying."

"House of..." Harper had tears running from the corners of her eyes.

"I was like when are these... *assholes...* gonna *go* somewhere. I was so angry. Then I finished the book, and I was just... so pissed, you know? Like how can they make an entire book where nothing happens? Then I closed it and looked at the cover. Plain green, white letters, just like the spine. I guess it was some abridged version for younger readers, but that wasn't the worst thing."

Harper wiped her eyes and waited with bated breath.

"The title of the book. It was Great *Expectations...* not Great Expeditions. You ever seen a book fly?"

Harper burst out laughing and put her wine down before reaching out and pulling herself against me, holding her face against my arm in a similar way to how she had buried her face against my chest when she first walked in. When she got herself under control and looked up, she cracked up all over again.

For my part, I was so happy I could have burst. To hear her laughter, to see a smile on her face and know I put it there, felt like first prize in a meaning of life contest.

I knew it was a stop-gap, though, a temporary thing. What happened to her in that group home was hanging over her every step of her life. I wished I could figure out how to make it all better.

Chapter 20: Harper

After hearing about Nick's adventures with Great Expectations, I thought I might not need an ab workout for at least a week. My stomach hurt by the time I'd calmed myself down.

The stress of my run-in with my mother seemed far away by the time we went to bed, and that was a relief. I thought it would bring me down for days until I caved in and agreed to go to the reading on Monday, even if there was no way I'd ever agree to break up with Nick on her say so.

Nick had said that his experience alone was probably a good enough reason to not do the Great Expectations movie, but even more important was that if I didn't want to do it, then I shouldn't.

It seemed so obvious, so logical, when he said it. It was hard to understand the way the fear of abandonment crept up on me and sent chills down my spine when being around him made me feel so warm.

He was right, but I had no idea how my mom would take it when Monday came and I didn't go.

*****

It was pitch-black middle of the night when I awoke to feel Nick's hand stroking my hair, his fingertips tracing down my neck, across my shoulder and as far down the side of my body as he could reach. I let out a contented but sleepy sigh. If he was feeling frisky, it surely was an inconvenient time.

"Mmmph. What's up?" I said.

"Just making sure you're still there," he said in a low voice.

"Where else would I be?"

"I like reaching out and feeling you there."

If I was a cat, I would have purred. I smiled in the darkness and stretched out before resettling myself, feeling sleep slowly taking over again.

"When I was overseas, wherever I slept, I used to reach out. Reach out for Christie. I knew every curve of her body by memory and I swore I could feel her reaching back to me. I hoped, somehow, she could feel it too," he said.

I opened my eyes, though it made no difference to how much I could see, and held his hand against the side of my face, pausing it at the beginning of another stroke. His voice was calm, but I could feel the faintest hint of a tremor in his hand.

"I bet she could," I said.

"When I came back and found out what happened to her, I... I still reached out every night. Stupid, huh?"

"No. Not even a little bit."

"After I left Warfields, I was in a motel somewhere one night and I... I just stopped reaching out. I couldn't feel her anymore. It felt like I lost her all over again."

"I'm sorry," I said.

"It's OK. I mean... it's not, it'll never be OK, but... now when I reach out, I feel you there. I love you, Harper. I love you."

"I love you too, baby. And I'm right here. And so are you."

I snuggled up close with my head resting on his arm. Nick stroked my hair again until the steady rhythm of it helped me drift off to sleep once more.

Chapter 21: Harper

"No. For the last time, no," I said.

"Harper, don't be silly now, tell him to leave because you've got work to do," said my mom.

"I'm not doing it. I'll be back later if you want to help me with some Dark Fox lines."

"What am I going to tell Goodman? He's a very important director. If we pull out, he's never going to work with you again!"

"You're my manager, right? So manage it."

I slung my handbag over my shoulder, opened the door, and tried to close it behind me, but my mother blocked it and followed me outside. Nick was waiting in his car, not too far from the bottom of the steps.

"Harper, come back!" she said.

"See you later, Mom. I love you."

I stepped into the passenger seat and put my bag down between my feet. Nick looked from me to my mom and back again while she gave us a look that could have killed an elephant at two miles.

"Everything... OK?" he asked.

"Not so much. I was supposed to be going in to read for Great Expectations today. My mom's not taking it very well. Can we get out of here?"

Nick pulled away and I felt my muscles unclenching one by one as he drove us down the street. I'd never seen my mother so angry and had no idea what she was going to do.

"She seems pretty intense," said Nick.

"That's a good summary. Anyway, forget about it, you've got me all morning so are you ready to tell me what you're going to do with me? You've been so tight-lipped I figured I had to bring everything to be prepared or give up and bring nothing, so I decided it was easier to bring nothing."

"That'll be enough."

"You're not taking me to read for Great Expectations, are you?"

"*Hell* no," Nick laughed.

Nick headed east along Santa Monica Boulevard and I kept on expecting him to look for parking at any moment, but instead he turned on to the South Hollywood Freeway. I teased him about perhaps being lost when he started heading north again on Alvarado. When he pulled on to Eagle Rock Boulevard, I struggled to keep up my end of the conversation. This area wasn't just away from my usual haunts, this was one place in Los Angeles I *never* went.

Somehow I knew, before he made the last turn, exactly where he was taking me, and I barely even looked up when he spun the steering wheel. Instead, I stared between my feet at my handbag, breathing but hardly feeling the air go into my lungs.

When I felt the car start to slow down, a hot flush raced upwards from my chest and quickly faded, leaving a thin sheen of sweat that felt suddenly icy cold despite the sun shining in through the window. I could see my legs shaking, an almost imperceptible quiver.

Nick had brought me to the worst place there was for me, the Tipton Group Home. I couldn't look at him. "Not here. Please, not here."

The voice I heard was barely recognizable as my own. It was weak and had almost regressed to a childlike timbre. I shut my eyes, lest I catch a glimpse of the house I knew was just to my right.

"Why did you bring me here?" I forced out, with no small measure of accusation.

"Harper, look at me."

I felt Nick's hand on my shoulder, almost on the back of my neck, and shied away from him for a moment, but there was nothing but care and gentleness in his voice, nothing but love in his touch. If there was one thing I was sure of in the world at that moment, it was that Nick was safety.

That was the only thing that gave me enough assurance to open my eyes and turn my head, mercifully away from the view out of my passenger window. The cool blue of Nick's eyes held my gaze so I couldn't look away, washing away the festering little notion that he might have brought me here for some cruel purpose.

"Believe me when I say that I understand what you're feeling right now," he said.

"No, you don't. You can't understand, or you wouldn't have brought me here. Why, Nick? Why?"

"I do understand. This place is your own personal hell. I have one of those too, it's… Christie's grave. Or the place where her parents had the memorial service anyway. One day I want you to visit there with me."

"This doesn't make any sense, Nick. Please take me away from here." The first tear fell from the corner of my eye, and I could feel the reinforcements on their way.

"If that's really what you want, then we'll go. You're safe, OK? OK?" Nick waited until I nodded before continuing. "Just listen for a second. This last couple of months with you has saved my life, Harper. When I first opened my eyes and saw you, I thought you were an angel. And I was right."

"I didn't save your life," I said.

"You did. You showed me there was still something good in the world, something worth getting up for every day instead of getting up out of habit. You gave me a reason to face the past, to face reality. Now the future doesn't seem like some crappy dark unknown wasteland, it feels like a place I'd actually want to be one day."

For a moment, his eyes seemed like almost a literal window to the soul. I could practically see the future myself, all the kisses, all the embraces, all the talking in the dark until we couldn't stay awake any longer, new homes, babies. Growing old. It didn't look so bad at all.

"But you've got this thing hanging over you, Harper. This idea that you must be some kind of trash because of what happened when you were barely more than a baby. Because of this place." Nick pointed behind me, but I still didn't look. "I want to help you face it."

"How? I just barge in there and ask for the current address of that... that woman who used to work here? Will you kick her ass?"

"No. I figured we could start out here and track down your birth parents. That's what really hurts, isn't it?"

The feeling that I wasn't getting any air came back, and I heard more than sensed that my breaths had become quick and shallow as I bordered on hyperventilating. That was a scary prospect.

"Isn't it?" he repeated.

I nodded. It did hurt, it hurt a hell of a lot.

"So I called here and talked to the guy who manages the place, seemed like a nice guy. I didn't know where else to start and he couldn't give me many details over the phone, with me not being you and all, but he did say that they still have records from when you were here. From when you were 'placed' here, he called it. He checked while I was on the phone and said there was even some property that belonged to you still here."

"What property? I didn't own anything."

"He couldn't tell me, but when I talked about the possibility of you maybe visiting, the guy practically begged me to make it happen. He asked, if you were up for it, if you could spend some time with the kids, because it would be so inspiring for them to see what somebody who used to live here made of herself."

"I don't know if I can even go in there, Nick. How inspiring is it going to be for them to see me faint?"

"You don't have to go in there, remember that. If you go in it'll be under your own steam, but I'll be with you. Think about it a bit, they don't even know we're here yet. He just gave me a list of times that *weren't* good, otherwise we could come whenever we wanted. If you want to go in, I'll send him a text and he'll get back to me. Hey, if that lady still works here, want to see me put her in a triangle choke?"

I looked down, a token smile barely lifting the corners of my mouth. This place had been the stuff of my nightmares for as long as I could remember. I never dreamed about monsters or the boogey-man under my bed when I was growing up. If my subconscious wanted to make me wake up crying, it just put me back here.

It had been a part of me for so long that the concept of being free of it was almost ludicrous. It couldn't happen, could it? What would going in there change? Nick was right though, what happened to me did taint everything else, a life I academically knew I should be overjoyed about. I had a family now, I was successful at a job that was sometimes stressful, but which I *did* love.

What's more, I was *in* love. The idea that the future I'd just glimpsed in Nick's eyes might be tarnished by this too if I didn't try to deal with it was what finally made me turn my head and look at the Tipton Group Home for the first time in over a decade.

"OK, I'll do it," I said.

Chapter 22: Nick

The way Harper was walking, all bunched up with her arms wrapped around her front, hugging herself, she looked like she was being led to the electric chair, but she was being so brave. I kept my hand on her back, gently urging her forward but trying to not cross the line from supportive to pushy.

When we arrived at the front door, I paused before pressing the doorbell to check in with her one last time. She was looking up at the window on the second floor furthest to the right. Maybe that was her old room.

"You ready?" I asked.

"I guess."

The 'ding-dong' of the bell inside made Harper flinch, and I saw her actually bunch her fists when the door first swung open inwards. However, standing just inside the doorway was about the most disarming thing imaginable.

A little dark-haired girl wearing what looked like official Princess Sundancer fairy wings was looking up at Harper with nothing short of hero worship. Her jaw dropped when she first opened the door, then opened and closed a few times as she tried to get some words out.

Further back, I could see a man and a woman waiting with a few other girls of various ages, wearing big smiles. The girl in front of Harper finally found her tongue with no small amount of effort.

"H-hello M-miss. Bayliss. On b-be-behalf of the T-Tipton Group Home and a-all the Seven F-fairy Kingdoms w-we… we thank y-y…"

The dark-haired girl burst into tears, the waterworks almost seeming to squirt out of her eyes like a cartoon. Her little downturned face jolted Harper into action and she swooped down and gathered the little fairy up in her arms, lifting her up into a hug that she would probably talk about for the rest of her life.

As the man and the woman came forward, I could see Harper whispering something in the girl's ear, but I couldn't hear what. She wiped her eyes and nodded.

"What's your name?" asked Harper.

"Kaylee."

"Wow, what a pretty name. I like your wings."

"Th-thank you," said Kaylee.

"Sorry Miss. Bayliss, Kaylee here is without a doubt your biggest fan in the world. I think she knows every song and dance in the whole movie," said the woman. "It wouldn't be safe for anybody to sleep here if you visited and she wasn't allowed to be the one to answer the door. I'm Regina, and this is Jeff."

Regina shook hands with Harper, and then Jeff extended his hand to her.

"I'm basically in charge of administration here," said Jeff, "Regina is in charge of the children day-to-day. Is this your bodyguard?"

"Nick," I said.

"Oh, *you're* Nick? Well, thank you very much. I'll be the smuggest manager at the next meeting when I tell them about this. Come in, come in."

We stepped through the door and Kaylee wriggled out of Harper's arms, her shock at meeting her idol apparently done with as she grabbed Harper's hand and begged her to come look at a picture she had drawn. Harper looked at Jeff and Regina hesitantly.

"Only if you have time, Miss. Bayliss," said Jeff.

"Please?" said Kaylee.

"Um, sure. Just call me Harper, OK? The place looks so different. It used to be so... clinical."

"Oh yes. Ideas have changed a lot about just how important a child's early environment is. We try to make it as non-institutional as we can. Staff turnover is absolutely *glacial* compared to the early days. That continuity of care is incredibly important. Regina here has been around for ten years, for example. I've been here for six. We both came after your time, sadly," said Jeff.

"You gotta see!" said Kaylee, leading the way and dragging Harper by the hand.

Kaylee brought us to a room with lots of beanbags and some comfortable-looking sofas and armchairs. One wall was almost entirely dedicated to books of all kinds. The lower shelves looked a lot more colorful and much more chaotic than the higher ones.

A woman who looked to be in her early thirties was on the floor putting together a puzzle with some girls about Kaylee's age, while a slightly older girl played with some toys by herself. In the corner was a girl in her early teens, wearing mostly black, with some dark make-up and hair covering one eye. She was reading a magazine and listening to an iPod at the same time and barely glanced at us when we walked in.

"This is it," said Kaylee, pointing at one of many crayon drawings on the wall opposite the bookshelves. It was a classic stick-figures-plus-house-and-the-sun-in-the-corner type drawing.

"This is me, and this is Mrs. Able, she came to visit me and she's going to take me home. That's here," said Kaylee, pointing at the house helpfully.

Harper looked straight up for a moment, and I could see her features contorting with the effort of holding back tears. When she looked back down, her face was the very definition of joy and she beamed at Kaylee. "That's great!" she said.

"Yeah! Will you read us a story?"

Kaylee, picture forgotten for now, pulled Harper towards the bookshelves, and the mention of the word 'story' got the attention of the puzzlers, who looked to have recognized Harper but were too shy to say anything. A couple of them wandered over, and one of them tentatively pulled a well-read looking book from the bottom shelf.

"Uh… yeah, OK," said Harper, eventually taking one book from each of the girls before she was led to a chair at the 'front' of the room.

Harper looked at me and I braced myself for any signs that she was panicking like she had been on the brink of in the car, but instead she gave me a happy smile and flipped open the first book. Puzzles and toys were immediately forgotten, even if magazines and iPods weren't, and Harper held the half dozen or so little faces enthralled with her ability to control her voice and speak different characters with different accents.

Regina and the woman who had been helping with the puzzle took photos, and Jeff stood there beside me looking pleased with himself. Harper had just finished the last book when the girl at the back piped up.

"What are you even doing here? Your charity visit for the year? Another photo op so you can show what a nice person you are and sell more tickets? You are so full of shit."

"Samantha! You do *not* speak like that to anybody, let alone a guest. You apologize at once, you're already in enough trouble as it is!" said Regina.

"No, it's alright," said Harper. "Samantha, is it? I'm visiting because I used to live here. My family found me here."

Samantha looked like she had another few choice words, but halted when Harper stood up. The kids on the floor and in bean bags looked from Samantha to Harper to Regina and back again as if World War Three might be starting.

"Can we talk?" asked Harper, picking her way between children towards the chair next to a disgusted-looking Samantha.

"Read another story?" asked another girl, who was echoed by the others.

"Hey!" I said, pulling a conical princess hat out of a big box of costumes and putting it on. "I found my hat!" The kids looked at me in silence for a few seconds and then agreed, by some undetectable child-radio-frequency, that, yes, a man as big as I was in a princess hat was hilarious. They rolled around the ground as Harper sat next to Samantha.

"You're not a princess!" accused one of them.

"Says who?" I asked, kneeling next to the box. "What else of mine do you have?"

They rushed over, and during the next fifteen to twenty minutes they found a lot of stuff that was possibly mine, and I had to try it all on. Most of it didn't fit. The woman who had been in the room when we arrived pressed play on a little CD player and excused herself for a moment.

Harper and Samantha had a hushed conversation under the cover of the music, and I was only a little surprised when I saw Harper give the girl a hug at the end, a hug that was timidly returned at first, but gained in confidence before they released each other. I knew firsthand that Harper was a good listener. I supposed Samantha had just learned that too, maybe along with how much Harper really cared about people.

"OK everybody," said Regina, "It's time for lunch, can we give a big Tipton 'thank you' to Harper and Nick for coming to visit us today?"

A high-pitched and semi-synchronized thanks came forth from the kids, and Kaylee hugged Harper's leg. "Come along then, let's wash our hands."

The kids filed out, Samantha coming last, glancing up at me but otherwise mostly looking at the floor. Harper pressed close to my side and I put my arm over her shoulder.

"Thank you for coming, Harper," said Regina, "I think we'll be watching Princess Sundancer on repeat for the next week. You too, Nick."

"It was really nice to be here, you guys look like you're doing a great job. The girls seem so... happy," said Harper.

"Aw. I hope so. Bye."

Regina left the room, leaving us with Jeff, who stopped the music. "I really can't thank you enough for coming, Kaylee is going to be walking on air. I guess that just leaves your paperwork and belongings? I've made you copies of the documentation and gathered it all together. All I had was a shoebox, sorry, but it was about the right size."

"Yeah, Nick said something about 'property' but, you know, I'm not really sure what that was all about. What property, exactly, is it?"

"Well, mostly, it looks like letters addressed to you."

Chapter 23: Harper

Jeff offered me a private room to look over whatever it was he'd put in the shoebox for me, and I accepted. When the door clicked shut behind him and I was left with it sitting in front of me on the desk, I felt my chest tighten up and had doubts about whether this was a good idea or not.

"Do you want me to wait downstairs, or outside or something?" asked Nick.

"No!"

The word came out much sharper than I intended, as if he'd checked how I'd feel about him puncturing the life raft we were floating in. Nick nodded and stayed where he was, in the chair on the opposite side of the desk from me.

I reached into the box with a feeling of dread, as if I was being forced to put my hand into a lion's mouth. Whatever was in this box might hurt me just as much, maybe more.

The piece of paper on top was a birth certificate. *My* birth certificate, apparently. And it had names I didn't recognize.

Child: Harper Jelka Milovanovic, born April 21 1993, Los Angeles, CA, USA. Mother: Jelka Daliborka Milovanovic, born August 12 1969, Sarajevo, Yugoslavia. Father: Unknown.

My heart boomed in my ears and I felt hot in the face as if too much blood was being pumped through my body. I wiped my eyes with the back of my hand, not surprised that simply finding out the name of the woman who had abandoned me was enough to bring tears.

I looked at that one document for a long time, reading it over and over even though there wasn't much information before putting it to the side and hitching in a few breaths with my head resting on my hand, hiding my eyes for the moment. A lump in my throat refused to be swallowed away.

I sensed Nick lean forward with concern. "You OK?"

I nodded. "M-my mom's name was Jelka. Jelka Mi... Mi..." I looked at the paper again. "Mi-lo-van-o-vic. I might have been Harper Milovanovic. Father unknown."

I cried, thinking about who Harper Milovanovic might have been, what she would have done, and tried to keep up with the tears, wiping them away. It was an impossible task, so I just let them flow for a minute while Nick reached over and held my hand.

I sniffed in through a suddenly runny nose and tried to take a deep breath around that lump, trying to summon up the hatred for this unknown woman I always thought I might feel if she turned up on my doorstep. Hate wasn't there though, it just hurt. It *hurt* so much. Sliding my hand out of Nick's grasp, I looked in the shoebox again. Now sitting on top was a stack of about a dozen envelopes, maybe more. I grabbed them all at once and began flicking through them, my pulse racing faster and faster when I read the words on the front of each one.

My lips pulled back in an ugly grimace, baring teeth that I thought might begin to crack at any moment from the force I was clenching my jaw shut with. A wave of grief not so much washed over me as smashed me against the rocks, and I let out a strangled gasp that bordered on a quiet scream.

The pain transcended the realm of emotions and cramped my stomach, making me hunch over slightly. The envelopes were labelled rather than addressed. I blinked rapidly and wiped my eyes, trying to clear my vision, and looked at the writing on each one.

Sweet Sixteen. When you fall in love. When your heart is broken. When you lose a friend. High School Graduation. Wedding Day. The birth of your first child. When you doubt your dreams. So many of them. One was simply titled *Munchkin* and had a big number one circled in the top right corner.

I pulled that one out and let the others stand in a toppled stack next to the box. What I held in my hands absolutely terrified me. I looked at Nick as if for some kind of reinforcement, but there was nothing he could do beyond sit there and offer silent support. If I was going to fight this battle, I was going to have to fight it myself.

The envelope was slightly yellowed with age and when I slid my finger under the flap, the nearly-two-decade-old glue offered only token resistance. The folded paper inside was only marginally off-white and covered in densely packed writing.

With a nose that wouldn't stop running and quivering hands that made it difficult to unfold the letter and hold it still, I began to read.

*****

Dear Munchkin,

I don't even know how to start a letter like this. I don't know how to even talk to you now that you're big, practically all grown up. You probably wouldn't like to be called Munchkin for a start, but I hope you don't mind me saying it one last time.

*As I write this you're in your crib having a nap, letting me have
some rest. It feels so strange to be writing to you like this, when
I'll be blowing raspberries on your tummy in about an hour.
I left instructions that you were to be given this letter when you
turned twelve, so Happy Birthday Harper, I hope your day was
magic and your new family made you feel like the special girl I
know you are. I guess by now they aren't so 'new' anymore. I
hope they fill your days with love, though.*

*You probably know some of your history by now, but I wanted
you to have it in my own words. I wanted you to know how much
I love you, now and forever. I love you my baby, I love you, I love
you.*

*I came to America alone in 1992, a refugee because things were
not so good in Sarajevo where I was born. Maybe the world has
forgotten about it by the time you read this, but believe me when I
say it was truly terrible, something that should be remembered so
we don't make the same mistakes again.*

*Like a lot of the girls I met when I moved to Los Angeles, I had
stars in my eyes. I could be an actress or a model, because I used
to do some of that back home. Like a lot of the girls I met, I
ended up being a waitress while I waited for my big break.*

*One day a man came in while I was working and flirted with me.
He was so handsome, so charming, and said all the things I so
desperately wanted to hear. I was only with him one night and
then I never saw him again. It turned out that the name he gave
me was false.*

*The best guess was that he was some man travelling to Los
Angeles on business and he took advantage of a silly, naïve girl.
That's me. I had dreams of being so much more though.*

*Almost nine months later I met you for the first time, and you
met me. It was scary being a single parent in a foreign land with
no family or friends but plenty of neighbors that didn't like
hearing a baby crying in the middle of the night through their
walls. Very scary.*

But I wouldn't give up. When you came into my life, you didn't end my dreams, you gave them meaning. You were the very reason to even have dreams.

All I ever wanted was for you to be proud of me, to give you everything you needed and wanted, to keep you safe. I kept on trying to get roles, sometimes I even had to bring you to auditions! I never landed anything more than being an extra in the background though. It's a tough business, but the worst of it was how much I worried you might be disappointed in me when you grew up.

With your help, I almost landed the role of the witch in a movie called Princess Sundancer. I'll never forget you helping me with my lines. You were dressed up in your little fairy wings waving a magic wand at me and saying "Kazoosh! Kazoosh!" as I read my lines to you. Do you remember that?

So close, but the lady in charge of casting said I didn't have the right look for the witch. It wasn't long after that that I started feeling unwell.

I fought and fought and fought. I'm still fighting, but I still have lung cancer. I don't have anybody to help me look after you, and I can't give everything a bundle of energy like you needs right now. That's why I decided I had to leave you in a group home. I visited ten of them, and I hope I made the right decision with Tipton. I made them promise to tell you all the time, it wasn't because I didn't want you, it's not because you're not my whole entire world, it's not because you're not the most loved little girl that ever walked the earth.

I'm having surgery soon. There's a chance that I might get better, that I might beat this. If that happens, then I'm coming for you, baby, I promise Mommy is coming for you. I'll pick you up and never let you go, I'll burn this letter and all the other letters I'm thinking about writing. I hope you never read this.

I might not beat it. The doctors use big words and promise nothing. That's why I'm writing this, and why I will write the others. So maybe you can know me a little bit, maybe I can be there on all those special days a mother is supposed to be there, so you never feel totally alone.

It's not fair. None of this is fair. But I won't stop fighting for you, Harper, right to the end. If it comes to that. They say the last thing you see before you die is your whole life flashing before your eyes, but for me I hope it's just going to be you, looking at me for the first time, and me looking back.

I love you so much. Be good. Have dreams.

Mommy

Chapter 24: Nick

Watching Harper read that first letter was heart-breaking. She went from bright red when she was fighting to hold back the sobs to having most of the color drain from her face when she couldn't stop them anymore and she read on.

To look at her, you would have guessed that a terrible horror movie was playing out on the piece of paper in front of her. Finally, with eyes all red and puffy like she'd been hit with a mild pepper spray, she folded the letter and put it back in the envelope as delicately as if it might disintegrate at any moment.

She packed all the envelopes and the other piece of paper back into the shoebox and stood, holding it to her chest and staring straight ahead. Her gaze seemed to be fixed somewhere in the distance. Even though she was looking right at me, I wasn't even sure if she was seeing my face. All she said was 'take me home'.

I tried to put my arm around her shoulder when I opened the door for her, but she shied away We passed Jeff in the hallway but Harper didn't even pause to say goodbye, heading straight for the stairs.

Thankfully, he seemed to understand completely as I made the briefest of apologies, explanations, and farewells on behalf of both of us. Maybe he had to deal with people looking up their pasts semi-regularly as part of his job, and maybe it was always an emotional experience.

The whole ride back to her house, I couldn't get a single word out of her. She just held that box against her chest like it would fly away if she didn't and stared ahead with those eyes that seemed focused on something only she could see. She looked broken, and I had major misgivings about whether my big idea to help her had been a good one.

Harper undid her seatbelt and stepped out of the car the instant I came to a full stop in front of her house. "Do you need me to come inside?" I asked.

"No."

"Oh. OK. Harper…"

She closed the door, not angrily, just in the same fashion she was doing everything else. Zombielike, as if she was going through the motions but hardly comprehending anything. I wound down my window. "Harper. Call me later, OK? Or I'll call you. I love you."

She walked in her front door and gently closed it behind her without saying anything.

*****

For two days, I didn't hear anything from Harper. When I went to her place, the gates were locked and there was no response from the intercom.

I tried to kill time with trips to the gym, with grocery shopping, with a few hours at the gun range. I cleaned my apartment from top to bottom again. Most of the time, though, I sat on my couch wishing Harper was there and hoping she was OK.

On the evening of the second day, I felt my phone buzz in my pocket and heard the beep of the text notification. That phone was whipped out faster than a six-shooter in a duel. It was a text from Harper.

'You home?'

I replied that I was, and a few moments later her message said she was on her way and she would be here soon. Thankful as I was to hear from her, the complete radio-silence for the past couple of days had me on edge.

There was no telling what had been in those letters, no telling what Harper had been thinking or doing since Monday. Had her thinking gone as far as reconsidering her feelings for me? Had my dumb idea traumatized her out of love? Panic stations.

In the brief time between buzzing her up and the knock on my door, the creeping sense of finality bloomed like an awful flower. My apologies were flowing out of my mouth before the door to my apartment was even fully open.

"Harper, I'm sorry. I'm no therapist, I didn't know what I was talking about taking you to Tipton, it was a bad idea. Are you OK? Tell me you're OK…"

Harper reached up with one hand and put a finger over my lips, stopping my ramble mid-plea. I saw she was carrying her overnight bag and dared to hope. It was so good just to feel her touch again.

"Shh. Take it easy," she said. "I'm OK."

"What… what about us?"

"What do you mean?"

"Are *we* OK?"

Harper's brow furrowed for a second, and then her touch moved from my lips to caress my cheek. "Yes. Yes, we're fine. I'm sorry about the last couple of days, Nick. That visit, all those letters, were really hard for me to get through. I feel like I've been in a daze since Monday. Uh… can I come in?"

"Of course."

Harper ducked under my arm, and I closed the door behind her while she put her bag in my room. When she came out, she slipped her arms around me and rested her cheek against my chest. The butterflies in my stomach settled and I hugged her back for a moment before she turned her head up to me, fixing me with those dark eyes that still made my knees weak. "You don't even know what you've done, do you?" she asked.

"No."

"I found her."

"Who? Your mom?"

Harper gave the tiniest of nods, her eyes never leaving mine.

"Really? Is she still in L.A?"

"Yes, but she... she isn't alive. I found her grave. I visited it."

"I'm sorry, Harper."

"So am I. But not for me. All this time I thought... well, you know. I was so ready to hate her, hate both of my parents, if they ever tracked me down. Anything would have been better than secretly hating myself for whatever it was that made them wash their hands of me. You're right. Tipton was my hell and I guess, in my mind, my parents were the demons."

"But, remember, it's not..."

"I know. I know. I do. It's OK now. I didn't just find her grave, I found *her*, too. She's no demon, she was a girl, a young woman, a real person. She wanted something better for herself and for me. She was a fighter. Someone who loved all the way."

Harper's eyes took on a glassy sheen.

"She was a mother. *My* mother, Nick. You gave her back to me."

Tears fell simultaneously from both of her eyes and I quickly wiped them away with my thumbs, my hands on her cheeks. Even upset, she was beautiful.

"I'm sorry I scared you over the past few days," she said, "I love you, and you'll have to try harder than that to get rid of me. I love you, I love you."

Chapter 25: Harper

Going to the Tipton Group Home and seeing a warm, nurturing, environment with mostly happy kids was a welcome surprise. I vaguely remembered when I lived here and so-called important visitors arrived, we had to line up and not speak unless we were spoken to. I didn't make the association at the time of course, but what it had really felt like was lining up for a firing squad.

That Kaylee girl was a little sweetheart. I was so happy she was going somewhere she was looking forward to. Samantha had had a hard life and was walking a fine line between hope and hopelessness.

She said she was too old to be adopted now. People who adopt kids as their own still seemed to want to *raise* them as well. I didn't know whether that was true or not, it certainly sounded like a possibility though. Regardless, she thought she was going to be in the home until she turned eighteen and then she had no idea what her place in the world was.

Against the advice of my mother's voice in my head, I had given Samantha my number and told her she could call me if she ever wanted to talk some more. I wished there was more I could do, I just hoped she didn't spread my contact details around.

With everything that happened immediately afterwards and in the following days, I had to have a good think when the text arrived asking if this was really my number and signed by somebody named 'Sam'. I confirmed and told her it was the first day of filming for Dark Fox Two, so I'd be away from my phone a lot but I'd always get back to her.

At first it was really tough to get back into character, into any character for that matter, but as the days and weeks progressed, I felt like I was back to normal. Better than normal, actually.

The ground I'd walked on my whole life had always seemed shaky at best, but now it was solid. I knew where I stood. Once things settled down, I felt a surge of confidence unlike anything I'd felt before, regardless of how well my movies or my performances had been received by critics and fans.

Acting can be an embarrassing job. Sometimes when you're in these awkward situations, saying things that sound cheesy, with wires and safety harnesses and crew members everywhere, you think there's no way this could be any good.

To give the best performances, you need to have no shame and throw everything you've got into it. To scream, punch, kick, kiss, love, cry, and strut like another person, you have to let it all go and for the first time ever, I felt like I could really do that because the ground would definitely be there when I came back down.

The magic of the job was stronger than ever, and I felt like I was doing exactly what I was born to do. I was being what Nick's friend, Sex Change Steve, would have called his 'true self'. I wasn't only fulfilling my own dreams, in a way it felt like helping my birth mother realize her dreams too. And I was over the moon, slow-motion-running-through-a-field-of-flowers, in love. That couldn't have hurt.

The fight choreographer loved some of the moves I was able to pull off and some of the ideas I had, but with the movie filming officially started, my training sessions with Nick were over. Of course, these days he wasn't my trainer, he was my boyfriend and everybody knew it, so we didn't need the excuse of Jiu Jitsu training to see each other.

Nick had a key cut for me so I could come and go in his apartment as needed, in case he was ever out working or at the gym or anything else he might want to do. With my mom, my adopted mom, quietly smoldering with misplaced indignation, I spent as many nights at Nick's place as I did in my own house.

I couldn't bring myself to tell her, or my dad and Orson, about having tracked down my birth mother. I didn't know how to broach the subject with things as they were between us. Every time I came home, I hoped things would have smoothed themselves over, but they didn't.

My dad did his level best to remain neutral, having always refused to be a part of the Harper-Bayliss-Movie-Star family business, and my mom always framed her rants in terms of the effect on my career rather than the fact that my relationship with Nick was my personal life. That kept my dad pretty much out of it.

Orson seemed to be siding with my mom more as time progressed, though never to such an extreme level. Maybe he felt like his role as unofficial security was being undermined by Nick, maybe he was just Big Brother protecting Little Sister. I didn't know.

I did my best to put it out of my mind. Something would have to give, but until I could figure out the right combination of words that would make everything right in the world, I had more than enough that was absolutely perfect to concentrate on.

One of those things was Nick's birthday, and I wracked my brains trying to think of what to get him for the big day. A quarter-century seemed like an important milestone, but he was a tough one to buy for.

The idea came to me when I was randomly browsing the Internet on my phone while in my trailer. An article was saying studies had shown that spending money on experiences, rather than material things, made most people happier in the long run.

It had something to do with the fact that we tend to look back on things like holidays with rose-colored lenses and remember all the good things about it rather than the long waits at the airport or the missed connections or carrying luggage everywhere. With material things, like buying a new car, it tends to wear down with time and the reality of having it there, rusty and needing repairs, brings us down more than the old memory of the thrill of a new car brings us up.

Then I remembered something that Nick told me on the night of the Fans Choice Awards and realized I was in a truly unique position. It was an insane idea, but surprisingly easy to organize.

Chapter 26: Nick

The future. It was something I hadn't had any reason to think about in such a long time. I'd been wandering around aimlessly for months before Harper came along and, for all intents and purposes, the future simply hadn't existed for me.

Now though, it felt like there were decisions that mattered beyond the next breath and the next meal. My plans from a year ago were out the window. I wasn't going to be career-military.

Could I live in L.A.? Sure, I'd go anywhere where Harper was, but doing what? The few hours I got with Johnny working on Jeremy Holt's security team weren't really enough.

Not that there was really any issue of making ends meet with Harper raking in untold millions per movie, but I needed to feel like I wasn't just riding on her coattails. A long-term plan wasn't easy to come up with.

I talked to Johnny about maybe starting up a security business of our own. With our know-how and Harper's social circle, we might have been able to get some pretty good contracts, but he liked the haven of having a billionaire boss.   Plus he enjoyed all the cool gadgets and innovations he got to see as part of his job, or occasionally play with, like with that license plate software he showed me.

Other people were unlikely to pay me what Harper had for Brazilian Jiu Jitsu training before we became an official 'thing'. I couldn't take her money when so much of the sessions got tied up with rolling around on the floor kissing her.

What's more, other clients weren't likely to pay for hiring the gym space either. Taking that into account, it was probably a long way away from a profitable venture. It would also be difficult to attract students as a purple belt when there were so many more highly qualified, and even famous, instructors already in the area.

Still, it wasn't like the pressure was really on yet, and compared to the bleakness of before, these felt like good problems to have. I had plenty of money left over from the sale of my parents' house, and it would last a while. Hopefully until a good idea struck me.

For the time being, regardless of the unknowns of the future, the present was a hell of a happy place to be. For example, Harper was up to something for my birthday.

I tried to think of where I was for my last birthday and struggled to remember what exactly had happened. It was possible that somebody was shooting at me though. This was much better.

All week, whenever she stayed at my apartment, she was all mysterious. She wouldn't let me book a restaurant or anything, she said she had it all under control.

Tonight, she actually kicked me out of my own home, saying she needed about an hour to sort out dinner and she hated other people being in the kitchen when she was cooking. I went on a meandering walk to the closest store to get a bottle of wine and took my time getting back.

When I returned, I tentatively opened the door a crack and sniffed the air, searching for some clue as to what Harper might have made. I smelled precisely no food whatsoever, nothing except her faint perfume.

I pushed the door open further and stepped in, seeing no evidence that Harper had done any cooking. What she *had* done was set up a lot of scented candles and turned the lighting way down.

"Hello?" I said, and received no immediate answer. I put the wine in the fridge and walked towards my bedroom. I was almost there when a sultry voice spoke from the shadows in the corner of the living room.

"I expected more impressive headquarters for a criminal mastermind like you, Marine."

A match flared for an instant, lighting up the pair of dark eyes I knew so well, before it was set to another candle, which she put on a shelf before extinguishing the match with a dramatic puff of air. The candle gave just enough light to reveal that standing in the corner of my living room, leaning with her back against the wall and one foot braced against it, was none other than Dark Fox herself.

Her face was partially hidden behind a thin black mask and framed by that glamourous brunette hair. Dark make-up highlighted her lips and eyes, the former curled in a smirk and the latter watching me intently. The black and grey top was strapless and skin-tight, dipping low at the front but otherwise in the style of classical Greek leather armor. Separating her top from her skirt was a belt with the Dark Fox logo front and center, but I glossed over that due to the view slightly lower.

Her boots came up to just over her knees and her bare thighs disappeared under the hem of that short skirt, showing just enough skin to set my heart racing. With one foot cocked up against the wall, her skirt was riding up even further than normal and I was almost disappointed when she dropped it to stand at full height and began to saunter towards me.

Harper strode like she was on the catwalk, each foot crossing the line of the other one as she stepped, giving her a sexy sway. She took her time closing the small distance between us.

The transformation was insane, like the night of the Fans Choice Awards but so much more extreme than girl-next-door to movie-star. She wasn't just the Harper I knew and talked to every day, she wasn't even Harper all dressed up for a big event, it was like she was channeling another person entirely.

The outfit itself probably helped. It was obviously custom-made from some portion of the hundred-million dollar movie budget and far beyond what any normal person could rent from a costume store, but it was so much more than that. Her mannerisms were different, the *attitude* of every movement was different, and the trademark Dark Fox sexual and physical confidence that bordered on arrogance was *all* there.

"What's the matter? Cat got your tongue? Didn't think I'd find you?" she asked, and pushed up on my chin with one finger, making my mouth shut with a click of teeth.

Harper put her hands on her hips defiantly with elbows way back, which pushed her chest out towards me. I wanted to throw her on the couch right there and then, climb between her legs and take her hard and fast... but something told me I'd have a lot more fun if I played along.

"How *did* you find me?" I asked.

"Pffft. Please. Did you really think you could try to poison me and I wouldn't beat your location out of one of your goons?"

"Poison?"

"Don't play dumb with me, Marine. This look familiar?"

Harper shoved some blister pack of pills against my chest before turning, sashaying away, and then bending at the hips, pretending to be very interested in something on my coffee table. Her skirt rode up, revealing tantalizing extra inches of her long legs. The view must have been so close to the bottom of her ass, it was all I could do to keep my hands off of her.

I looked down at the blister pack in my hands, and I swore my heart stopped beating for about five seconds. These weren't some movie-prop cyanide capsules or something. These were birth control pills, with several already gone from the packet.

"Are these your plans for world domination?" she asked, apparently commenting on my National Geographic magazine. "Amateurish. Like your attempt on my life. There's not a poison on this planet that can hurt me," she finished, standing up and turning to face me.

"Well done, Dark Fox. You survived the poison, you found my hideout. It's such a shame you'll never leave. Such a shame you'll live out your days here as my plaything."

"Oh really?"

"Really."

"Well, let's see if you fight as well as you talk."

Harper narrowed her eyes and adopted a fighting stance. I cracked my knuckles and did likewise.

Chapter 27: Harper

My fighting experience was pretty much limited to movies where people were paid to have the stuffing knocked out of them by my character, but when Nick flexed his muscles and bunched his fists, he looked ready to kick some serious butt. He looked so dangerous, so freakin' sexy, but I maintained a mask of indifference, because Dark Fox wouldn't have been impressed.

I loved the Dark Fox character. Putting on these clothes was like flicking a switch. That part of the role was *easy* to act out because when Dark Fox's timid alter-ego put on the costume, I felt what she was supposed to feel.

It was sexy, it was powerful, and it was absolute self-assurance. I felt like I could do anything.

I aimed a slow roundhouse kick to the right side of Nick's body, expecting him to block it. Instead, he trapped my leg with his arm curling around the back of my knee and spun us both to his left, where my back hit the wall next to his bedroom door with a thud that rattled the generic art that Nick's landlord had hung up. There was hardly any time to let out an 'oof' before Nick's whole body was pressed up against mine, pinning me against the wall. My lips pulled back in a snarl as I ineffectually pushed against his shoulders, moving him about as much as I could move a mountain.

My left leg was still up in the air, held with my knee just above and behind his hip, and I felt Nick's hand gently slide up my thigh until he was squeezing my ass under my skirt and he discovered the one piece of the Dark Fox costume I hadn't put on. The piece designed to protect my modesty when I did high kicks.

Nick let out a quiet breath through an open mouth and, if we were animals out in the wild, I would have said the look in his eyes meant he wanted to eat me all up. I kept pushing against him in a mock effort to escape as he slowly and deliberately moved his hand inwards, never taking his eyes from mine, until his fingertips brushed against my bare sex and he found out just how turned on I was.

If the hard bulge pressing against my body was anything to go by, he was just as crazy with lust as I was. I let out a shuddering breath as he gave me one gentle teasing stroke before letting my leg go, still keeping me pinned against the wall.

"What have you done to me, Marine?" I growled.

"You should be more worried about what I'm *going* to do," he said in a low voice.

Nick grabbed both of my wrists, keeping just enough of his weight leaning against me to hold me where I was, and lifted my arms slowly above my head. I struggled to stop my arms from being raised, helpless against his strength.

"It can't *be*," I said.

"You're *mine*, Dark Fox," whispered Nick into my ear when he had both of my arms pinned above my head, crossed at the wrist and held in place with just one of his big hands.

Nick reached down and caressed my leg again, sliding his fingers up my outer thigh and pushing my skirt up at the same time. Short as it was, it fell back down when his hand reached my navel.

I could barely feel his fingertips through the material of the Dark Fox costume, but when he squeezed my breast, there was no missing it. A shiver of anticipation broke my super-heroine defiance for a moment, but I did my best to recover.

"You'll never get away with this, Marine," I said.

Nick didn't respond, he simply moved his hand up, over my chest and neck, curling his fingers around the back of my neck and pulling me into a kiss that cut off all my comic book bravado. I couldn't stop a satisfied sigh escaping mid-kiss and by the time our lips parted, I had to pant for air.

He let go of my wrists, and I didn't even have the presence of mind to move them before both of his hands were on the back of my thighs and lifting me up in the air with him between my legs. Nick pressed close and I could *feel* him against me, pushing against my most intimate place.

Moving as if I weighed nothing, Nick leaned back and pulled me away from the wall before stepping to the side and pushing through the door to his bedroom.

The sensation of him moving between my legs spoke to some primal part of my brain, making it scream out in need, and I gently rocked my hips against him as I held on to his shoulders to steady myself.

Nick glanced down at the bed and saw the last element of this little game, some fluffy pink handcuffs attached to the headboard. He looked at me with a raised eyebrow, and I felt him pull me against his hard bulge even more intensely for a moment.

"That's cute. You think you can contain me here," I said, looking back at the restraints.

We fell to the bed with Nick on top of me for a moment before he shuffled upwards to straddle my stomach. I pushed against his abs, his chest, for a few sweet seconds before he took each of my wrists in turn again and secured them in the cuffs.

I tugged against the handcuffs, the metal rattling against the headboard despite the pink padding, and looked at Nick with confusion.

"What are these made from?" I asked.

"Antiumbravulpinium, of course," he said.

"No…"

"I told you, you're *mine*, Dark Fox."

Nick slid his fingers along my cheek and buried them in the hair at the back of my head, pulling my head to the side so my neck was bared to him. He licked and sucked my naked skin, moving towards my lips before kissing me deeply once more.

I was lost in the kiss and immediately forgot about the handcuffs, which rattled again when I tried to wrap my arms around him. The frustration, the longing, was surprisingly intense. I wanted to feel him, *needed* to.

"Do your worst, Marine," I challenged. "I'll never talk."

The corner of Nick's mouth rose in a smirk. "Oh… you'll squeal," he promised.

Nick crawled backwards off the bed, climbing off and standing at the foot as he pulled off his shirt to reveal that chiseled physique I couldn't get enough of. I wanted to run my fingers over every hard muscle, kiss all over his body, but I wasn't going anywhere.

I tried to sit up, and the handcuffs pulled my arms back as I strained towards him. My legs were straight, the toes of my boots reaching out to try and touch him but not quite able to when he took his pants off and stood before me in all his naked glory. His manhood jutted out straight and hard and would have been an almost intimidating presence if I didn't want it so bad.

The last bastion of Dark Fox's token resistance was dismissed when Nick climbed back on the bed and pushed his hands between my knees, parting my quivering legs and leaving me defenseless to anything at all he wanted to do. I was his, just as he said, and I was crazy for him.

When he lowered his mouth to my sex, he made good on his promise. It wasn't long before I squealed, and then squealed again and moaned in blissful abandon as he took me exactly where I needed to go.

It was wonderful torture. I wanted to run my hands through his hair, over his body, but I couldn't. I did everything in my power to bring us together, curling my legs, bucking my hips, pushing against the headboard. He moved with me, keeping me on the razor edge between not-enough and too-much-to-handle, until I couldn't take it anymore and moaned with reckless abandon as my climax hit me.

Finally, he moved between my legs and I felt him at my entrance. No condom, nothing between him and me. Nothing but my bad boy and his captive heroine.

His sound of satisfaction when he slid inside was a stroke to my ego, and Nick wasted no time in taking every ounce of pleasure he could from me. His every move was as urgent as if the end of the world was coming and he wanted to feel every part of my body before it happened.

The whole bed shook with his movements. For all I knew, the whole world might have been shaking. Nick sat up, still moving inside me, and I felt his hand on my neck, squeezing firmly but nowhere near painfully as he controlled the pace.

I held on to his arm, held on for dear life, and came again as he hit a furious rhythm. My toes curled in pleasure inside my boots when I felt him let go in my depths, when he took the final part of a gift I'd never even come close to giving anybody else.

I completely lost track of time as we panted and did our best to catch our breath, a sheen of sweat on both of our bodies. Nick stayed inside me as the afterglow enveloped us and he kissed me tenderly in contrast to the wild devouring of before.

It might have been a wordless minute later, or an hour, when we were silently staring into each other's eyes, me still hiding behind the Dark Fox mask and make-up.

"Is that all you've got, Marine?" I whispered, utterly spent.

"Where's my dinner?" he asked, and we both fell to pieces laughing.

Chapter 28: Harper

After an awkward chat the next day with my friend in Wardrobe, I found the details of a drycleaner the studio had a standing non-disclosure agreement with and took the Dark Fox costume in for an emergency service and an even more awkward chat. I wished I could have delegated that job to somebody else but, by the next day of shooting after the weekend, it was thankfully ready to go.

My mom and brother became more distant, which put a damper on what otherwise would have been the most perfect time of my life. Perhaps the distance was because I was so busy shooting and so there was a lot less for my mom to schedule and negotiate on my behalf than during those between-movies times, but that only drove home the notion that at some point, I'd traded a mother for a manager.

The filming was going smoothly. I got the impression that everybody was having the same feeling I was, that we were making something that was truly great. It was something that would be received as not just a wonderful comic-book-adaptation, but simply a wonderful movie.

Sure, there were times when I missed the good old days before I turned eighteen and they couldn't legally expect me to work more than a certain number of hours or after a certain time at night, but it was a small sacrifice to make for that exhilarating feeling that I was pouring my soul into this larger-than-life character, creating something that people would respond to.

When the director, Jay Garnett, asked myself and several other cast members to stay late one night, I was pretty much obligated to do so, despite the fact that Nick and I had plans. I tried to reach him on his cell phone but it kept on going to voicemail.

I had to wonder if he'd left it at home before going out somewhere else on his way to my place, where he was supposed to pick me up this evening. He was always leaving his phone behind. Eventually, I had to get back on set so I left a message.

"Hi, it's me. Don't know if you'll get this in time, but I'll be running late tonight. I have no idea *how* late. We might have to postpone dinner. I've got to go, but I'll come back and check my phone when I can. Love you, baby."

I ended the call, dropped my phone, and was almost out of my trailer when I wondered what would happen if he *didn't* get the message and turned up at my house. My family was there and they still hadn't found a way to accept him yet. I bit the bullet and called my mom.

"Hello?" she said.

"Hi Mom, I'm just calling because I'm going to be late getting home tonight."

"Oh, you were coming home tonight?"

I paused, hurt at the icy tone. "Yes, I was. Briefly."

"OK, was there anything else? Need me to tell Garnett that you're not doing Dark Fox anymore?"

"Mom, get over it. I'm calling because I can't get through to Nick and he might be on his way to our house to pick me up."

"And?"

"And I need you to tell him I'm going to be late. Let him in if he wants to wait. Be nice either way."

"Harper, honestly, haven't you played with this boy's emotions enough?"

"What are you *talking* about?" I asked.

"Orson told me all about it."

"What does Orson know about anything?"

"He knows what you said to him," she said.

"Which was what, exactly?"

"That you're with Nick just to irritate me, as well as to satisfy some... some bad boy fantasy you've got..."

"Oh. My. G...."

"And, let's face it, he's with you for the status, so he can show off to his friends and..."

"Stop right there!" I yelled. "You haven't even tried to learn the first thing about Nick. *You don't know anything about him!* Orson doesn't have a clue what he is talking about..."

Somebody knocked on my trailer door and I heard the call that I was really needed back on set. I lowered my voice.

"Mom, Nick may or may not show up. If he does, you be *nice*. Please, don't put me in a position like that, don't make me choose."

"I don't believe what I'm hearing. After everything I've..."

The knock came on my door again, and I called out that I'd be there in a second. "I've got to go. Bye."

I dropped my phone again and left my trailer, following the guy who had come to track me down back to the set. Everybody was waiting for me, and I did my best to apologize and get on with my job.

It wasn't at all easy to get back into character. My stomach was churning with a mixture of anger and fear about what my mom had said, what she might do. I had a really bad feeling about this.

Chapter 29: Nick

That was a birthday to remember. In the days that followed, I kept on having flashbacks to certain moments, and I suspected I'd be having them until the end of my days.

It wasn't just the craziest, most satisfying sex I'd ever had in my entire life. It wasn't just the moments of hilarity or the magic as I watched her transform back to Harper Bayliss as she removed her costume and make-up.

The truth was that I'd never been happier or more deeply in love, but that was a difficult thing to admit to myself. In a way, it felt disrespectful or dismissive of the memory of what Christie and I used to have, because I'd loved Christie with everything I had too. Thankfully, with Harper, it was a difficulty I didn't have to go through alone. I brought it up later that night over the pizza we had delivered when she gave me a small birthday present. Something *other* than herself for me to unwrap.

It was a picture of us. Wallet-sized. I'd never had a picture of anybody but Christie and I in there. After everything Harper and I had done, for some reason, this felt like a daunting step.

"You don't have to take the other one out," she said. And that settled it. Harper and I stayed awake late, just talking and laughing in bed, and I stayed awake long after she fell asleep peacefully in my arms, just basking in the perfection of it all. Part of me wanted nothing more than to repeat that day over and over forever.

Unfortunately, wishes like that seldom come true. The world kept on turning and Harper had a busy schedule shooting the Dark Fox sequel. Between Harper, the gym, and the odd shift of security work, I kept as busy as I could too.

Tonight, I had an interesting idea of somewhere to take Harper. In my travels, I happened across a place called "Concealed Meals" where your food was served in absolute pitch dark and the waiting staff were all visually impaired. It had incredible reviews, so I went ahead and booked a table for two.

The danger of the place was that they didn't tell you exactly what you were being served, so it was a bit of a lottery in that sense. I didn't know about Harper, but although I wasn't allergic to anything, I also didn't *like* absolutely everything. That's why I decided to stop at the store and get some salted-peanuts or something to smuggle in so we were in no danger of starving.

I was walking down one of the aisles when the cover of a magazine caught my attention out of the corner of my eye. It was your typical brightly-colored sensational-styled trashy magazine, but the biggest headline on this one, aside from the title, was Harper Bayliss' Sizzling Bikini Pics, and sure enough, the cover shot confirmed she looked pretty damn hot in a bikini. I recognized it from our day at Manhattan Beach.

Although I was sure I looked altogether too similar to the people who perused those magazines at the very back on the *top* shelf, I couldn't help but look both ways before grabbing this one to have a quick look. The photos of our kiss had surfaced weeks ago. I wondered how many more were being printed now.

I found the page easily enough and saw that the photos were taken from a completely different angle to the previous ones, and they were a lot clearer. A different photographer with a different camera perhaps.

The pictures were, for the most part, about what I would have expected, Harper looking gorgeous and perfect as she splashed around in the water or sunned herself. The last one made my heart sink a bit though. Apparently the paparazzo was still there snapping away when Harper and I were getting ready to leave, and he'd caught me in the brief moment between when I took off my rash vest and put on a shirt. All my scars were there in crystal clear definition for the world to see. The caption read 'Beauty and the Bwaaaaaaaahhhh! Kill it with fire! Please don't touch our Harper, Mr. Martell!'

"Assholes," I muttered, and put the magazine back on the shelf.

I should have been used to it. People had been flinching at the sight of my scars for almost a year now, but every now and then it still took me by surprise.

The way Harper looked at me didn't just make my heart melt, it was such a relief from what had become the norm too.

It was almost like she didn't see the scars at all, except I knew she did because sometimes she would trace her fingers along them as if she was trying to touch each one in turn. The thought of Harper made it a lot easier to weather the looks from other people.

I patted my pocket and cursed. I'd left my phone at home again. It shouldn't matter too much, I knew exactly what time we had arranged, but I hoped Harper wasn't trying to get through to me with a change of plans because of working late or something. Still, there was nothing I could do about it now. If I went home for my phone, I *would* be late.

*****

When I pulled up in front of Harper's house, I waited for a minute or so. Every time I'd picked her up before, she had come rushing out before I ever had a chance to knock, whether I had to buzz the intercom at the gate or not. Come to think of it, I had never set foot inside her house yet.

Harper never came out and said it, but I got the impression that her family hadn't warmed to the idea of the two of us yet. I wondered if their sentiments were anything like that photo caption I'd just read.

The arctic glare from her mom when she opened the door told me that there was indeed no warming at all. Not the slightest bit of thaw.

"Nick," she said.

"Evening, Mrs. Bayliss. Is Harper home yet? I forgot my phone so I don't know if…"

"Let me get right down to it," she interrupted. "I don't want you seeing my daughter anymore."

"Uh… no offence, ma'am, but that's not really your decision to make."

"Listen. I, we all, appreciate what you did for Harper with that maniac, but you two just aren't right for each other."

"Why not?"

Mrs. Bayliss' eyes softened as if she was giving me what she considered a harsh truth that I needed to hear. "Your whole relationship is built on shaky ground."

"Mrs. Bayliss, I don't know what you're talking about. You might not believe it, but I love Harper and she loves me. That's all that matters, that's the least shaky ground there is."

"Does she? She *is* an actress, you know. A good one. I didn't want to be the one to tell you this, Nick. I've been telling Harper she needs to do the right thing and come clean."

"About what?"

"You two met under," Mrs. Bayliss threw her hands up, "extreme circumstances. So she employed you for some kind of training as an excuse to spend more time with you, but she told Orson she was doing it as some kind of rebellion against me and because she wanted to satisfy some... boy from the wrong side of the tracks fantasy. She's been using you, Nick. No offence, but do you really see a girl like Harper going for a guy like you?"

I looked at my feet for a few seconds. The words Mrs. Bayliss was saying were painfully plausible, stirring up the unavoidable fears that lurked at the back of my mind about Harper and me.

The past few months had been like a fairy tale. Was it possible that's what it literally was? In that brief moment, everything I could remember about the time we spent together flashed through my mind, those fears whispering that it was all true and if I looked hard enough, I'd find the evidence of her charade.

It all made too much ugly sense. Then I thought of reaching out and feeling her in the night. I could feel her even when she wasn't there. She was a part of me, and when I saw the way she looked at me, I knew I was a part of her too. She *was* an incredible actress... but she couldn't fake that. I looked back up.

"To put it mildly, Mrs. Bayliss, you are absolutely full of shit."

Chapter 30: Harper

When I pulled into my driveway, I was hoping to see Nick's car parked there in front of my house, but it wasn't. I hadn't been able to get through to my mom since finishing up for the night, and this was just one more circumstantial sign that something wasn't right. I stepped through the front door, listening for any sounds that would tell me where everybody was. I felt myself waver between fear that my mom might have told Nick what she had implied before and flashes of anger at the same possibility. What if she told him and he believed her?

The clearing of a throat and the dull clink of a glass being set down brought me to the living room, where Orson was reading a book and my mom was tapping away at her tablet PC, a bottle of wine sitting next to her glass on the coffee table in front of her. The way they both did their best to appear not to notice me was one more nail in the coffin of my hopes.

"What did you do?" I asked.

"You'll thank me one day," she said.

Blood rushed to my head and pounded in my ears as I circled around the couch, standing on the opposite side of the coffee table from her. My breaths came in quiet wavering gasps as I struggled to keep myself from screaming with rage.

"*What* did you *do*?"

"He's not good enough for you."

"Take it easy, Harp," said Orson, maybe seeing the shade of red I was turning.

"You. You shut your mouth." I glanced at Orson and then brought my focus back to my mom. "It's not the nineteen thirties anymore, if I want to be with Nick and he wants to be with me, then we're going to be together. So I'll ask again. *What did you do?*"

I was a nuclear reactor perilously close to meltdown. A bomb. A volcano. I felt my hands bunched up into quivering fists at my sides as I stared her down.

"I told him exactly what I said I was going to. He needed to hear it."

For about two seconds I was silent and still, somehow transported from the edge to the eye of the storm. Then the yelling started.

I had no idea what I even said, but I vaguely saw myself pick up the bottle of wine by the neck and throw it with all my might straight through the window over Orson's head. I wanted to punch something until my knuckles broke. I wanted to burn the house down.

The intensity of my anger was completely out of the ballpark of anything I'd ever felt before. The scenes that played out in my head were violent and frightening, and I understood crimes of passion for the first time.

I had to get out of there. I had to talk to Nick, and I had to get out of there.

Fumbling for my phone, I raced out of the room and headed upstairs. I slammed my bedroom door behind me and held the phone against my ear as I found my bag and started stuffing things into it.

I almost cried when I heard Nick's voicemail recording. I didn't even know what I said or if I left a message at all. My mind was that far gone.

How long ago had Nick left here? Did he, in fact, forget his phone at his place? Was he at home and avoiding my calls or was he not even back there yet?

These questions were all beyond me. I couldn't figure out what to do. I couldn't even think properly.

I spotted my iPod on top of my drawers and grabbed it, clutching it against my chest like some kind of magic shield. *A run. You should go for a run to think. If you go driving now, you'll just crash.*

Before I knew it, I was pounding down the stairs in my running gear, fixing the headphones into my ears and scrolling through my music looking for the two hours of thunderstorms. Orson, carrying a brush and shovel, spotted me at the bottom of the staircase.

"You're going for a run? *Now?* Hold up, I'll come with you."

"Stay away from me."

I slammed the front door behind me as the first thunderclaps played out from my iPod and the pitter-patter white noise of raindrops started. I jogged down the steps and paused by my car, staring at it with jaw hanging open at the sheer ridiculous luck.

The wine bottle I had thrown out the window of my house had apparently sailed straight through the right rear window of my car. I shook my head, threw my hands up, and then continued running.

Once I was through my gate and on the sidewalk, I sped away much faster than my normal pace, feeling desperate to get distance between myself and the people whom I could barely reconcile my love with at the present time. It was the end of a grueling day, and I couldn't keep that speed up for too long though.

My strides shortened and the shadowy world, poorly lit by a sliver of moon, passed by much more slowly. I forced my breathing into an even pattern, feeling my whirling brain begin to relax and unclench at the same time.

Energy was diverted from blind rage into the exercise, and I could almost feel the recorded rain washing away some of the more insane things that had crowded into my mind a few minutes ago. I wasn't calm by any stretch of the imagination, but I could at least think.

First thing was first. If my mom told Nick that I was only with him to annoy her and because I wanted to slum it for the while, how would he respond to that? I thought about the possibility of never being in his arms again and felt a lump forming in my throat, making it difficult to keep my breathing even. I still couldn't understand why my mom was so adamantly opposed to Nick. Why didn't she see in him what I saw?

The idea that everything we'd shared might be wiped out because of something I couldn't even comprehend was awful. Everything we'd shared. That gave me hope.

Surely Nick must realize he was more than some bad boy booty call. I'd told him my greatest fears, he'd shared his most painful memories, and we were still crazy about each other before tonight. We fit together like we were two pieces of the same person.

Whenever I fell asleep snuggled up against him, I slept like I was in the safest place in the world, and when I lost myself in his eyes, I could see him looking just as lost in mine. That couldn't be undone by mere words from my mother, could it?

I hoped Nick had told her that she was full of crap. After I returned from my run, I would go to Nick's apartment and I'd wait for him if he wasn't there. We would get through this. I promised myself we would.

That left the lingering problem of my mom. Her cold distance was bad enough, her active attempts at breaking Nick and I up were intolerable.

The fear of losing her, losing my family again, had never let me consider laying out an ultimatum like I was now contemplating, no matter how much she had controlled my life. I didn't want to do it, but I would. I would cut her out of my life until she accepted Nick. As I was trying to think of how I could word such a demand, a car accelerated past me before slowing down at the intersection ahead. It turned right off of my street and on to the street that I would have to cross to make it into the park, disappearing behind the wall that surrounded the property of whoever lived on the corner.

The street seemed even darker than before after the sudden flash of the headlights and I concentrated on the ground for the moment, not wanting to add a twisted ankle to my current list of grievances. The park was really well lit, so I didn't have far to go before I'd be clear of the shadows.

I didn't even see it coming. The impact made me think I must have been hit by a car. I couldn't hear anything over the white noise in my headphones until I hit the sidewalk, scraping my elbow painfully and jolting one earbud loose.

My wind had been knocked out of me at the first collision, hitting the ground made it all the worse, and now there was a crushing weight on top of me. And a man's voice. I couldn't make out what he was saying because one of my headphones was still in, half drowning the words out with rain and thunder, but he was scrabbling for my wrists, trying to hold me still.

With burning lungs, I went on auto-pilot from all the BJJ drills Nick had put me through and pushed first one of the man's knees downwards and then the other, putting him in my guard before I grabbed at his collar with one hand and gripped the sleeve of his shirt behind the elbow with my other. After putting my left foot on his hip to help me swivel my butt out to the side, I swung my leg in front of his face and pulled him into an arm-bar.

I held on to his hand for dear life and began stretching my body out, extending his arm out and then putting all the pressure I could muster from my whole body on to his elbow, straining to bend it backwards, to hyper-extend it to the breaking point.

The man grunted in surprise and pain and almost fell to the side on his back. That was a common reaction to this particular technique, Nick had told me, but after the tiniest of staggers he regained his balance and managed to get to his feet, pulling me up off the ground before suddenly dropping back down to his knees again.

My head bounced off the sidewalk with a sickening '*thunk*' sound that I felt more than heard, and I saw stars. I tried to hold on to his arm, tried to keep my knees together tightly to maintain the position, but everything was spinning.

I felt his arm slip out from my grip as my body seemed to go limp, and there was something warm and wet on the back of my head. The world swam for a moment and I couldn't hear thunder and rain anymore, all I could hear was the sound of my feet being dragged across the ground.

My eyes wouldn't focus, I barely knew which way was up when I felt myself stuffed into some small and cold space that smelled like gasoline and engine grease. Another '*thunk*' sound, much more metallic and much more external to my body than the previous one, plunged me into almost complete darkness for a few seconds before I both heard and felt a car starting up and the shift in momentum as it drove away with me inside.

I blacked out.

Chapter 31: Nick

Harper's message was borderline gibberish, but after playing it a few times, I managed to decipher that she was on her way to my place. Looking at the time of the missed call, I figured she might arrive within the next half-hour if she had left more or less just after hanging up.

She didn't. After forty-five minutes I called her phone, but it just went through to her voicemail. I supposed she must be driving and didn't hear it go off or something.

Another half-hour later, I couldn't help but be worried. I tried calling again, but she didn't answer and I didn't leave a message this time.

Listening to the voicemail she left me once more, she sounded really frantic. I hoped to hell she hadn't been in an accident.

It was just shy of eleven-thirty when I called and left a voicemail saying I was on my way over to her place to make sure everything was OK. I was just about to turn the key in the ignition when my phone played its little jingle.

I sighed in relief when I saw that it was Harper calling.

"Hello? Everything OK?"

"Nick?" a man's voice answered.

"Yes, who's this?"

"It's me, uh, Orson."

"I'm not in the mood for any more of you and your mom's bullshit right now, Orson. Where's Harper?"

"She's not with you?" he asked.

"No, why do you have her phone?"

"Shit, Nick. Oh shit…"

There was an edge of panic in his voice, one that I'd heard a few times in my life. My heart beat hard in my chest and I took a deep breath before speaking slowly and clearly.

"Orson. Listen to me. What happened?"

"Shit... shit... she was pissed and she went for a run by herself. I was only a few minutes behind her, I thought I might be able to catch up, but I found her iPod on the ground at the end of the street... and... oh *shit*..."

"And *what*?"

"Blood on the sidewalk. The police are all over it, but man, I was hoping maybe she tripped and hurt herself, flagged down a taxi or somebody and went to an A&E or your place. The police are checking with hospitals, but nothing yet."

I barely heard anything beyond 'blood on the sidewalk'. I'd heard those words once before, and they nearly killed me. This couldn't be happening again, it couldn't be like Christie all over again.

A sheen of sweat stood out on my forehead, and I leaned against the steering wheel as everything spun for a moment. For a few seconds I thought I might throw up, but the sensation passed as I fell back on my training, to keep rational under pressure, under absolute chaos if necessary.

When a person goes missing, for whatever reason, their chances of being found drop off a cliff the longer the search takes. I wasn't there when Christie needed me, but Harper had only been gone for an hour or two at the most. I would find her or die trying.

"Which end of the street did you find the blood?" I asked.

"Just opposite the park."

"So she would have run past the Holt place?"

"Yeah, why?"

"Maybe nothing. Keep Harper's phone with you, I'm on my way."

*****

Johnny started off by asking me what I was doing calling him at this time of night, but soon flicked the switch to business mode when he heard what was happening. As I was tearing along in my car, I asked him if he still had access to that license plate software. He did and I told him to meet me at the Holt Tower. He met me at the front doors about five minutes after I arrived and swiped us in with his pass card, taking me right up to his office. The computer seemed to take an infuriatingly long time to turn on.

"The police are already on it, of course?" he asked.

"Yeah, they're out there now apparently. I just want to see if the security camera outside Mr. Holt's house picked up Harper for a start, and then see if there were any cars driving around at the same time. Who knows, they might have seen something, we can get those details to the police so they can be contacted and questioned."

Johnny entered his password on the computer and the flat screen on his wall came to life, showing a duplicated display of his computer desktop. He clicked an icon and entered another username and password on a box that popped up, then began scrolling down a list that appeared.

"What time was it?"

"I'm not sure exactly, can you start at about nine o'clock and fast-forward through until we spot her?"

"Can do."

The display flicked to the view from the camera outside Jeremy Holt's house and a moment later, any moving objects on the screen, like cars, people on bikes, and some other couple out running together, began moving at high-speed. I narrowed my eyes, straining for any sign of Harper, and felt an electric jolt when she finally went past the camera in a blur.

"Back it up, back it up, that was her. Go back like five minutes and turn on that software. Give me a pen and paper, I'll take down the details of anybody that comes up."

"No need, I can just print it all off."

Johnny reset the video and played it at normal speed. Only a couple cars went past before Harper appeared, the little animated labels floating above them the same way I remembered from Johnny's first demonstration. Harper was running pretty fast and only stayed on screen for a few seconds, but nobody appeared to be chasing her or following her. About ten seconds later, a car went by driving slow and going in the same direction as Harper.

The label appeared above the car, showing the little hour-glass as the software pulled the information from wherever the hell it got it from and then showed the driver's license. I groaned as I saw the picture and leaned on Johnny's desk as an invisible iron band wrapped itself around my chest.

"What is it?" asked Johnny.

"That one. That's the guy with the acid! Bring it up again. Do it, *do it!*"

Johnny tapped at his keyboard and brought the guy's details up again. There it was, his address.

"How do I get there? *How do I get there?*" I yelled.

"I don't know, Nick. We should just give the address to the police, right?"

"Fuck that. I'm going straight there, you give the address to the police when I'm on my way. Bring up a map! Go! Go!"

Johnny copied the address, searched for it online, and then requested directions, which brought up a blue line showing the quickest way to get there from the Holt Tower. The printer sprang to life without me needing to ask.

"You got a gun here?" I asked.

Johnny opened up a cupboard behind his desk, revealing a safe, which he opened and reached in to grab a handgun. By the time I snatched the map with directions off the printer, Johnny was unlocking a small metal box he took out of a drawer in his desk that turned out to contain the ammo.

The former Marine sergeant ejected the clip and began loading it up for me with practiced speed. He double-checked the safety and handed it over.

"You be safe, Nick,"

"If he's hurt her…"

"Just go, I'll call the cops."

Chapter 32: Harper

The first thing to invade my confused dreams was the sound of somebody humming the theme song for The Last Perfect Day. The next thing I noticed was just how much my head hurt. It was especially painful at the back, but my whole head was absolutely pounding. I wanted to roll over and go back to sleep, except I realized I wasn't even lying down. I was upright in some kind of chair. With a groan, I opened my eyelids a crack and felt a jolt of fear that made my head explode with pain and brought up flashes of colored light in front of my eyes.

Something was very wrong, I wasn't home, and I wasn't at Nick's place... I didn't know where I was. I lifted my head, wincing at the pain behind my eyes and in my stiff neck, squinting at some man who approached when he heard me stirring.

I tried to blink away the blurriness of my vision and saw that he was maybe in his mid-thirties but had the kind of look on his face like he thought all his birthdays had come at once. Then I recognized him.

The last time I saw his face, he was wearing sunglasses and was trying to throw a cup of acid on me. When I tried to stand, to retreat from this madman, I found my hands were tied to the chair behind me and my ankles tied to the legs of the chair.

Everything came rushing back – going on a run and getting tackled in the darkness, being stuffed into the trunk of his car, and blacking out. I couldn't stop a whimper from escaping when he kneeled in front of me.

"Harper! Welcome back, you had me worried for a second there!"

His excitement was palpable. It was so out of place with the situation, like he had not the slightest inkling that he had done anything wrong. A man like that might do anything.

"Don't hurt me."

I was almost ashamed at the terror I heard in my own voice, like it couldn't even belong to me. I wanted the words to come out with confidence, but they simply didn't.

"Hurt you? I could never hurt you, Harper. I love you."

"You... you tried to attack me with acid, you knocked me out and tied me up here!"

The man looked pained and put his hand on my knee. I tried to squirm away, but there was nowhere to go with my hands and legs restrained as they were. He seemed distracted by the touch of his palm on the bare skin of my leg for a moment and I shuddered, which seemed to break him out of his reverie.

"About that... I'm... I'm sorry for calling you a bitch that day. I was out of line. You're not a bitch, you're the most wonderful woman in the world. You're just a bit confused."

"What are you talking about?"

The man stood, walked over to the wall, and I got my first chance to really look around the room. Posters from my movies wallpapered all sides. DVD and Blu-ray cases hung on the wall as if they were family portraits or art. Shelves were covered in what might have been movie props, and one area was dedicated to some kind of collage of pictures of me cut out from magazines.

Many things looked like they had been signed and he went to one of these, a little promotional poster for The Last Perfect Day. He read the message there, holding his finger an inch away from the words.

"To Walter, thanks for being my biggest fan! Love, Harper. Kiss kiss."

The man, Walter apparently, looked back to me with a big smile as if the message explained everything. Maybe prompted by my blank expression, he walked around a single bed towards some other piece of paraphernalia. Low on the wall next to the bed, I saw a picture of me from a trip to the beach the previous year when a wave had dislodged my bikini top, resulting in a good payday for some paparazzo. A hot flush rose to my head and seemed to increase the pressure there, sparking another jolt of pain as Walter pointed at something else.

"To Walter, glad you enjoyed the movie! Love, Harper. Don't you see?" he asked.

"See what?"

"I love you... and you love me. We were meant to be together. All the girls I ever knew ignored me or told me to drop dead, but not you. You're special."

"This... this isn't what you do to somebody you love, Walter," I said.

"Yes it... this is just a means to an end, though. You're so busy, it's hard for you to find time for me, and our relationship was suffering because of it. *I* was suffering because of it. I wanted to do something for you, for *us*. Something romantic, something to show you how much I love you. That's what the acid was about."

"Please don't hurt me, Walter," I repeated, feeling a fresh surge of terror at the mention of acid. He might have killed me with a rushed splash from a single cup in public, how much worse could he do with all the time in the world and me unable to run away?

Walter continued as if I hadn't spoken at all. "You're always surrounded by such shallow people. All those people that wait in line with me to see you at your signings when they don't even love you like I do. The whole world is shallow, they don't see you like I do, they don't see how beautiful you are on the inside, how deep. That's what I wanted to show you, I wanted you to see that I would still love you even if you weren't beautiful anymore. Isn't that romantic? Do you understand now?"

I didn't answer, I just looked down at my lap through a blur of tears.

"Then that big freak ruined it all and I haven't been able to get you alone to talk since then."

The mention of Nick broke my heart and a sob forced its way out of my mouth. I might die tonight, and there was still the possibility that he thought I was only with him to spite my mom. He was the love of my short life. If there was no way out of this, I hoped there was some way he could know that.

"Don't do it, Walter, I don't want you to do it."

Walter stood behind me and tried to wipe my tears away, but I flinched at his touch. The very feel of his hands on me made my skin crawl.

"Oh, Harper. Don't worry. I've had a lot of time to think about it, and I've come up with something even better."

He went to a shelf and picked up a long thin dagger with elaborate designs on the pommel that I recognized well. I should. After all, I had the original back at home. It was a replica of the weapon my character used to save the world in Those Lost Ones.

"Recognize it? You do, don't you? I was thinking... it would be a shame to ruin your perfect beauty with something so inelegant as *acid*. If I use this, it'll be as simple as a quick stab through the heart. You'll always be young, strong, beautiful. I'll bring you into my... *our*... bed and then shoot myself. We'll be together forever! Like Romeo and Juliet. They'll talk about us for hundreds of years! Don't you want that, Harper?" I tried to speak, tried to say no, but all I could do was shake my head, cry, and listen to my own horrified moans. *I don't want to die.*

Chapter 33: Nick

"Come on, you piece of shit."

My car didn't respond to the urging, the underpowered engine was already doing as much as it could, revving almost as fast as my heart was beating. If ever there was a situation where I wished I hadn't bought a car on a strict budget, this was it. I needed anything with more power. A tank or a monster truck maybe.

Wavering between blind panic and a desperate need to think clearly, there was one thing that kept my thoughts on track. Harper *needed* me to think clearly.

I'd be no good to her if I never made it to that psycho's house, so I forced myself to concentrate on the road. I tried to make sure I wasn't going to crash into anything or anyone but paid no heed to the speed limits. I hoped to catch the attention of a bunch of police and bring an entire convoy of them with me, but so far I hadn't seen a single one.

City lights whipped by on either side, first downtown and then more residential areas. I'd memorized the first part of the drive while I came down in the elevator, but there were a few lefts and rights that I would still need the map for near the end.

I could see the white of the paper my map was printed on out of the corner of my eye, weighted down by the gun on the passenger seat. A car, thankfully seeing the speed at which I was approaching the intersection, hesitated and I blasted straight through, hearing their horn change pitch as I raced past.

"No, no, no, no..."

My hands gripped the steering wheel tight enough to make my knuckles turn white. Try as I might to keep myself under control, there was an undeniable sense of the very worst kind of history repeating, and I muttered my denials through clenched teeth into the empty car. I couldn't lose Harper. I. Could not. Lose. Harper. The possibility of slipping back into that gray existence, that life without a future, was horrifying. I didn't think I could make the journey through that particular hell again.

The driver in front of me saw me coming and instead of getting out of the way, I saw the brake lights come on. I tried to move into the right lane to overtake them, but they moved lanes at the same time. I swerved back to the left, blasted the horn, and let out a stream of expletives that they couldn't possibly have heard.

The flush of rage at the other driver was like a tiny prod that started a snowball running down a hill, making my mind bounce and rumble ever more chaotically as it gathered speed and momentum, spinning crazily. Lights of cars and buildings alike took on a blurry quality, and I realized I was crying as the thoughts shouted for attention in my head.

I remembered when Harper came to visit me in the hospital, when she wriggled into my life and fit like we were made for each other. Her smile, her voice, everything she said and did was like a splash of vivid color that spread out from her and made everything heartbreakingly beautiful.

How could I see those colors and then have them taken away? How dull and derelict the world would look, like an abandoned city covered in volcanic dust.

"Don't take it away," I said to nobody.

I turned off the main road, the setting becoming more suburban with every building that swept by until it was all houses, most of which were completely dark. The occupants of those houses were probably sleeping peacefully, with no idea that the most important person in my world was at the mercy of someone who might hurt her. Or worse.

The streets were, mercifully, almost entirely abandoned by the time I was a few blocks from the main road. I took a left and then reached the end of the route I had managed to memorize before getting into my car. Without looking, I pulled the printed map out from under the gun and transferred it to my hand holding the steering wheel. Reaching up, I flicked on the cabin light and hurriedly stole glances at the page in front of me while still driving at breakneck speed down the poorly lit street.

I shot through one intersection and took a right at the next before dipping my eyes to the map again. Third on the right, that was Walter Lambert's street.

A terrible thought fought to the forefront of my mind. What if he hadn't taken Harper back to his house? What if he had somewhere else to go? What could I do then? I'd be as helpless then as when I'd come back to find Christie already missing for weeks.

I decided I'd jump off that bridge when I came to it. I had no choice really. The first thing was to get to his house, kick that front door off its hinges, and pistol-whip him to within an inch of his life if he'd hurt Harper.

If I was too late… there was no telling what I would do. Given enough time before the police showed up, there was the possibility that nobody would ever find Walter Lambert.

I squinted at the map in the dim light, trying to read the name of the last road on the right before I was supposed to turn off. Dabney Street.

Ahead, I could see the blue street sign and focused on it as I rushed closer and closer, praying I hadn't taken a wrong turn, that I was in the right place. It definitely started with a 'D'.

Dabney! I was close. My heart leapt and I forced the accelerator against the floor even harder, drawing just a little bit more gas into the engine. My car was momentarily lit up by the headlights of some other vehicle driving into the intersection from my left just as I crossed the stop line.

There was no sense of pain upon impact. The whole world just turned into blaring, crunching, screaming, metallic noises. My vision seemed to whirl, I had no idea if my car was in an uncontrollable spin or if I'd been hit on the head.

I caught a glimpse of my lap covered in little pieces of broken glass, then my car slammed into something on the passenger side and everything fell into silence. Warm fluid flowed down the side of my face and I fumbled for the release on my seatbelt for a moment before a dark fog flowed in from the periphery of my vision. I was still desperately searching for the button when the fog covered everything I could see and I went numb.

I was so close.

Chapter 34: Harper

From somewhere in the distance, the sound of screeching tires was quickly followed by a couple metallic crunching sounds before silence resumed. Walter, who had just begun to advance on me with the dagger in his hand, went to the window and peeked out from between the curtains.

I almost cried out in relief at the delay, like a prisoner in the electric chair who sees the executioner with his hand on the switch go to answer the phone. I gasped in hitching breaths, pulling desperately at whatever was tying me to the chair and only succeeding in making the binds dig into my skin even more.

Walter turned back to me and shrugged. "Dumbass kids again. They're always racing around in the middle of the night, drunk or high or something. It was only a matter of time before they had an accident. Not our problem."

"I don't want to die! I don't want to die!" I sobbed.

"No! No, no, Harper, you've got it all wrong. This is how we live forever. You and me."

"You're crazy!"

Walter's face changed about as quickly as if a button had been pushed somewhere, his hopeful smile disappearing as his lips thinned and his brow furrowed. "You... you be quiet! You sound just like *them*... it's... you've... you hit your head. I cleaned it all up because I love you. You hit your head, that's why you're talking like that."

I looked on in horror as he came at me with the dagger, pushing backwards against the chair as if there was somewhere to escape to. The thin knife glinted in the light and Walter circled to my right side before dropping to one knee and putting his left hand on my shoulder.

He pressed the tip against my chest. I could feel the sharp point through my shirt, poking against my skin just below my sports bra. It may have been a replica of a movie prop… but it was probably going to be all too functional.

I squirmed and sucked in my stomach, knowing how futile it was but unable to stop myself from trying to get away. There wasn't going to be any moment of calm, any last defiant look. Dignity was out the window. I wanted to *live*.

I wanted to live and see that future I'd seen in Nick's eyes. The future was supposed to be *ours*. He gave me back my past and I wanted us to have our future. It wasn't fair! We were so *close* to it.

Walter hesitated. "From what I've read, this should be quick and painless as long as I get it straight into the heart. You should hold still."

My head slumped forward and my eyes squeezed shut as the hopelessness of it all washed over me, threatening to wipe out my inner light as surely as a dagger to the heart would. Then I thought of Nick. I thought of my birth mom.

They would fight to the end for love, tooth and nail, with everything they had. But what did I have? I opened my eyes to see the dagger still pressed against me, Walter taking deep breaths to psych him up just to my right. I had one thing left. Maybe.

Do it, Harper. Do it if you want to live. You're an actress,
right? So act. Or die. My internal monologue had never
been so blunt before, but it was right. Act or die. I
blinked and shook my head as if clearing the cobwebs.
"Wait," I said, looking at Walter with dawning
recognition. "Walter?"
"Huh?"
"I'm sorry, Walter, I didn't recognize you. I hit my
head? It hurts."
"Yeah. Yes… uh… you did."
"Sweetie, I'm so sorry."
Walter looked like a dog that had just been petted for
the first time in its life, wary but unable to stop its tail
from wagging.
"Sorry about what, Harp?"
"All this." I nodded at the dagger. "You're right. Of
course you're right, it's so romantic. We'll be together
forever. Like Romeo and Juliet. But there's just one
thing…"
"What is it?"
I leaned my head over and raised my shoulder, bringing
the back of his hand to my cheek. Walter looked
mesmerized and licked his lips.
"It's just that, well, we've waited so long, Walter. We've
waited *so long* to be together. Shouldn't we… enjoy
ourselves for a while first?" I asked.
"What… what do you mean?"
"We should go somewhere, like a honeymoon… don't
you think?"
"A honeymoon?" Walter looked like somebody who
had prepared a Valentine's Day dinner for a new
girlfriend but forgot to ask first if she was a vegetarian
or not.

"Yeah. I've always dreamed of going away somewhere, just you and me. Somewhere nice, away from the crowds. Somewhere we can just be ourselves, talk about everything, maybe spend some days in bed..." Walter almost visibly broke out in a sweat when I said the word 'bed', and I felt the tiniest bit of pressure relieved from the tip of the dagger as his lower brain processed what that might mean. My skin crawled as I watched his eyes traverse my body, almost as if I could feel his gaze like fingertips on me.

"W-where would we go?" he stammered.

"Oh... some deserted island maybe? I'd pack almost nothing but bikinis. Let's go, Walter. Tonight. Now?" Walter's hand slid from my shoulder to my chest and I fought against every instinct to flinch away, instead pushing my breast against his palm.

"Yeah... all of that... just cut me loose and we'll go now, OK?"

My captor's eyes drooped shut, and his lips parted as he savored the sensation of what he was feeling, something he'd probably imagined a thousand times or more. He pulled the dagger away and wiped the corner of his mouth with the back of his hand before standing up and moving behind me again.

"We'll go! We'll go!" he said.

"Yes, Walter, I love you! We'll go now! Just cut me loose!"

My excitement leaked into my voice. I couldn't help it. I might have bought myself a bit more time. I might have bought myself the freedom of my arms and legs. I might have bought myself a chance. The blade of the dagger slipped between the skin of my wrists and whatever was restraining me, cable ties maybe.

I waited for the sweet release of pressure around my wrists, but it didn't come. Walter held the dagger there for what felt like a million years.

"Wait a minute. You're just tricking me…"

"No! No, I mean it! Let's run away together, please…" An open-palm slap from behind caught me completely unaware and made my ear ring as it rocked my head to the side. The dagger was pulled back, and I felt the sting of a cut on my wrist.

Walter paced to the other side of the room near the window, his hands over his ears, breathing heavily. His face was almost as red as my blood that now stood out bright on the blade. He was muttering something about me being just like the others.

I tried to regain his trust, stay in character, salvage the scene, but I was too scared. The feeling of hope, so close but snatched away, robbed me of the thin veneer of co fidence I'd been relying on to *almost* pull it off. I was still pleading with him when he dropped his hands to his sides and looked at me with murder in his eyes.

"Shut up. We'll die tonight. Together. And in time, you'll learn to love me. Nobody else needs to know what you tried to do."

He advanced on me again, and I couldn't think of anything else to do but try to keep the images of Nick and my family in my mind. There was a hell of a lot of unfinished business in my life, but I wished things hadn't ended on a day like this. I hoped they all knew I loved them, really. I loved them so much.

Chapter 35: Nick

'Harper Bayliss Found with Throat Slit.'

I was staring at a newspaper headline, unable to believe it. Below it was a picture of Harper, Harper as she should have been. Harper as she was such a short time ago. Young, beautiful, perfect, a soul that cared so much for other people. For me.

The words of the article seemed to shift and move around every time I tried to read them, every time I tried to read about how I failed. One second they said one thing, the next they said another. I had to start over again and again.

People were talking to me, saying things that didn't make sense. Why wouldn't they leave me in peace to read this newspaper from my nightmares?

"Man, where you learn to drive? I called the cops, they go'n arrest yo ass. Hey, you alive, man?"

The newspaper faded away and I opened my eyes, vision and pain both rushed back into my existence at the same time. I was in my car with my head resting against the steering wheel. It was night time.

I sat back, watching the dashboard sway and swirl for a few seconds before turning my head to the left and looking into a couple of faces that were showing a mixture of anger and concern. I had no idea who they were.

"What happened?" I asked.

"You drive like a jackass, what happened," said some guy that looked like he might be in his late teens.

Get to Harper, a voice in my head screamed. I gasped, which sent a spear of pain into my side. I reached around and grasped at my ribs with a grunt. At least one of them was surely broken.

"How... how long was I out?"

"Like a minute," said the other guy.

I turned my head and fought back the nausea as the entire world kept on whirling when I stopped. The gun was no longer on the passenger seat, I couldn't see it anywhere.

"Shit."

"Damn right."

The piece of paper with the map printed on it was miraculously still on my lap. I picked it up and blinked at it a few times, trying to bring it into focus. My thumbs smeared blood on the paper as I held it, but I finally managed to read and recall the number of Walter Lambert's house. It should be one block ahead and one house from the corner on the opposite side of the street.

The seatbelt release, so elusive before I blacked out, clicked easily and I tried to open my door, only to find it jammed shut. The door on the other side was pressed up against a parked car, so I began to climb out the window.

"Hey, what you doin', man? You need to stay there. We ain't letting you go."

I crashed to the ground and cried out at the explosion of pain from my side, as well as the sickening sensation of everything spinning while the broken ends of my ribs seemed to grind together. It took three attempts, but when I rose to my feet, I towered over the two of them and they didn't look so confident in their abilities anymore.

"Here." I gave them the map with Walter's address on it. "The police are already on their way. If they stop to talk to you, send them here."

"You late for a party?"

"I better not be."

I began lurching in the direction of Walter's house, leaving the two confused young men in my wake.

Every breath was punctuated by a spark of pain as my lungs inflated against however many broken ribs I had, and every time I put weight on my left leg, it hurt, but that pain at least eased with every step I took.

By the time I reached the next corner, I was already jogging, my leg hurting but almost fully functional, though every time I inhaled was still agony. There it was. The only house I could see on that side of the street with a light on. One room at the rear-left side of the house.

Adrenaline surged through me and dulled the pain of my ribs. I picked up speed and nearly sprinted across the road, heading for the front door. I kicked it with everything I had, right at the edge and just under the door handle, throwing my entire weight behind it and pushing off my planted foot.

It didn't come off its hinges, but the door jamb was effectively splintered and the door crashed open against the internal wall. I ran through the nineteen seventies décor in the direction of that room at the far left of the hallway, barging through the door with a voice inside my head screaming and begging that I would find Harper there, and find her safe and sound.

I burst into a room almost entirely covered in movie posters and pictures of Harper. It was a shrine to her if ever I'd seen one, but more importantly, she was there. She was tied to a chair with blood dripping from her fingers behind her, but she was alive.

Standing in front of her, in the middle of the room, was Walter Lambert with a long thin knife in his hand and a dumbfounded look on his face. I didn't give him time to think. I barely gave myself time to think, relying on my experience of being in situations where people were trying to kill me.

Walter had no such experience and swung the blade in a wild and uncontrolled arc, missing me completely and allowing me to grab hold of his wrist as I drove him backwards into the corner of the room. He hit the wall with a thud and I drove my shoulder into his mid-section, hearing the wind get knocked out of him even as the pain in my ribs blossomed anew.

"Nick!" Harper screamed, seeming almost delirious with stress.

I extended my legs and felt the top of my head hit Walter's nose with a satisfying crunch as I pulled back on his wrist and then slammed it against the wall again and again until the knife was dropped. With that safely on the floor, I created a little distance between us and aimed a knee to his stomach that doubled him over before pulling him backwards and tossing him towards the ground.

In the distance, I heard sirens approaching and almost laughed in relief. This nightmare was almost over, but Walter wasn't out for the count yet. I needed to subdue him until the police arrived.

He was already trying to sit up when I trapped his head and right arm between my legs and put him in a mounted triangle choke as I knelt over him. In a few seconds, Walter would be unconscious and I could find something to restrain him without the danger of him fighting back or recovering that dagger.

Walter's right hand tried to grab at my face, but he couldn't reach. He arched his back to try to get me off of him, but that wouldn't have helped his case even if he did manage to roll on top. The blood would be cut off to his brain just as well with me on the bottom. The hold was locked-in.

When the gunshot went off, I realized my error in judgment. He hadn't arched his back to try to dislodge me, he'd done it so he could reach for a gun he had tucked into the back of his pants.

My ears were ringing, and a whole new spear of pain was thrust into my belly while the rest of me went numb. Walter's eyes finally lost focus as he was choked unconscious and I managed to glance down to my right where his arm now hung limp with a revolver loosely clutched in his hand.

The triangle choke was still on tight, held on by my own body weight, as I slumped forward until my face mashed ungracefully against the ground, looking towards the wall. A warm river flowed out from my side, and I felt like some kind of hydraulic machine with a leak. I couldn't seem to make myself move.

The sirens came closer and closer, and somewhere behind me Harper was screaming something. I couldn't hear what that might be. If Walter was to be released from the choke now, he'd regain full consciousness in less than a minute and still have that gun in his hand. If it stayed on for another few minutes, he'd have brain damage. A few more minutes and he would be dead.

In a way, I was glad that the decision about Walter Lambert's life was out of my hands. It was all I could do to concentrate on the dust and lint on the floor in front of my face. Disentangling myself from him was completely beyond me. *I'm fucking dying*, I thought.

'No'. That's what Harper was yelling. Over and over again. As that damned dark fog rolled in from the edge of my vision for the second time in too few minutes, I tried to muster up all my strength for one last thing. I just wanted to turn and see Harper safe.

Come on, Marine, you want the last thing you see to be this dirty floor? Move! My head barely twitched.

The last time I thought I was going to die, I was in a foreign land thousands of miles from anybody that loved me. As the darkness covered my eyes completely, I could feel Harper reaching out to me across the few feet that separated us like a comforting hug, and I thought that this was almost alright.

Times like this would get you thinking about what the meaning of your life was. Over there, I didn't have an answer to that question. I wished I hadn't left home. This time I thought maybe I was put on this earth so that Harper could *stay* on this earth. That was OK by me. The sirens and screams warbled and buzzed in my ears, seeming to become distant as another sound became clearer. I heard a voice echoing from my memories. It was Harper.

I'm right here. And so are you.

I didn't feel any anger or fear. Maybe I didn't have any energy left for that, maybe it was because she was with me.

I love you so much, Harper, I thought at that beautiful memory.

I love you too, baby, it said.

Chapter 36: Harper

Before I opened my eyes, I reached out to the other side of the bed. Nick wasn't there of course, but I hoped he could feel it anyway.

It was lonely, waking up all by myself back in my room in my own house, but I'd take it over waking up tied to a chair. I stayed in bed for several minutes, letting the sounds of birdsong and the distant whir of a lawnmower slowly chase away that last bit of sleepiness. There was no filming schedule to keep to. The scenes that required my presence had been postponed for as long as I needed to mentally and physically recover from my ordeal. As long as that didn't take more than a month or so. So, for a few minutes at least, I could take my time.

Today was a big hurdle I had to get over, though. There was nobody else to do it, so I set the date myself. This was one of those days where I'd look back and think of my life before now and after now as two almost-separate things.

Eventually I couldn't put it off any more, and I swung my feet out of bed, determined to face this daunting thing. When I went downstairs, I found my mom in the living room, sitting in the same spot she had been on that awful night, with her head leaned right back and her fingers interlaced over her eyes and forehead.

"Mom?"

She dropped her hands and turned to look at me, and I saw that she was wearing exactly what she had been wearing the previous evening. Could she have been there all night? The bloodshot tinge to her eyes hinted at that very possibility.

"Are you OK?" I asked.

"I don't know. It's… every time I start to nod off, I start hearing these sounds like somebody's trying to break in. Doors rattling, tapping on the windows, footsteps. I've sprinted halfway up those stairs at least three times overnight thinking somebody might have gotten to you."

Tears fell from her eyes and I circled the couch to sit next to her, pulling her into a hug. After a moment I felt her arms around me, squeezing once and then releasing as she sat up straighter.

"Look at you," she said. "After all you've been through, and it's me that's a mess. How are you so strong, Harper?"

"It's a hell of a strange thing, thinking you're about to die, then to not have it happen. I feel like… I don't know. There's so many possibilities now compared to when he was coming at me with that knife. I thought about you, you know. When I thought it was the end. You, Dad, Orson, and Nick. All the people who showed me what home, family, and love was all about. All the important stuff. I was so sad about how we left things, I just wanted you to know that I loved you. That's all I felt, so much love."

"Harper, I love you too… you know that, right?"

"I know… but we've had some problems lately, haven't we?"

My mom clasped her hands on her lap and looked down at them, suddenly unable to meet my eyes. She nodded without glancing up.

"It's not even all the stuff with Nick. Everything changed after The Last Perfect Day. I feel like I haven't seen my mom since then."

"What do you mean?"

"Since then, you've been my manager. Where's the mom who used to read me stories before I went to bed? Where's the mom who said I could quit acting tomorrow if I felt like it? Where's the mom that told me we'd just go get some ice cream if I did? Something changed, and I don't like it."

My mom looked up for a fraction of a second before dropping her gaze again, wringing her hands together anxiously. She took a few deep breaths before answering.

"I'm sorry... I... I didn't know what I was doing. I *don't* know what I'm doing. It's tough being a parent. You start off with this helpless little thing who needs you for everything, then one day they don't seem to need you for *anything*. Overnight, it was like you were suddenly all grown up and riding this wild bull of a career. I saw a way I could be... useful? I don't know... a real part of your life for a bit longer anyway. I just didn't want to lose you."

"Oh, Mom. How could you think I didn't need you?" She shrugged and I reached out to take her hands. "I tracked down my birth mother, you know."

That brought her head back up with an almost audible snap. "When? Where is she?"

"A little over a month ago. She's... she's dead. But even if she wasn't, you'd still be the one who brought me up, you'd still be the one who was always there for me. I always thought that my birth parents threw me away like a piece of garbage. No matter what, there wasn't a day that went by that I didn't remember that and feel a little part of me get torn off. I know better now. I *needed* to know better, or one day there wouldn't have been anything left of me to tear off. I need you to be my mom again too."

"OK… of course. I…"

"And that means you can't be my manager."

My mom looked as if I'd told her the world was coming to an end. "But… but… Harper, I… you need to have people you can trust to…"

"I want to be able to talk to you about my job. I want to be able to talk to you about my personal life. I want your advice, but I want it as my *mom*, nothing else." I gave her hands a squeeze. "Mom, I love you so much, but this has to happen or, one way or another, you *will* lose me. I have to be my own person, and I can't do that with you as my manager."

"Are… are you firing me?"

"Think of it as a promotion."

My mom looked past me out of the newly repaired window for several seconds before meeting my eyes again. "OK. I don't know what I'll do with myself, but OK."

I hugged her again. "I love you, Mom. Thank you. I'm going to have a quick breakfast and then I'm gonna head out."

"Where are you going?"

"You know where."

Chapter 37: Harper

If I thought people were interested the first time Walter attacked me and Nick saved me, they were absolutely frothing at the mouth over this one. It was a media-frenzy.

So great was public interest that there had been police stationed outside our house twenty-four hours a day for the last few days, just making sure people kept their distance. Flowers and messages of support were all over our fence and littered the sidewalk on either side of the driveway.

I met Nick's friend and boss, Johnny, the day after the night at Walter's. At his insistence, he'd recommended one of his guys who was qualified for freelance security to stay with me as much as possible until I could figure out how I was going to handle my bodyguard situation in the future. The police repeated their earlier recommendation for such measures.

My temporary bodyguard, Bryant, had been staying in the guesthouse since then and kindly doubled as my driver this morning. When we arrived, for the first time in I had no idea how many years and despite how many people were there waiting for me, nobody asked for an autograph. There was nothing but people yelling encouragement. Bryant didn't even have to do anything but follow me.

When we went upstairs and down the hall to the right room, Bryant waited at the door while I went inside. I stepped around the curtain and saw that he was already awake, staring out of the window at the morning sky with a day-dreamy kind of look on his face.

My heart just about exploded with happiness, it felt like it was swelled up to double the normal size and I didn't have enough room for it anymore. The pressure of it seemed to lift the corners of my mouth, and I couldn't stop myself from breaking into the silliest of grins.

"A penny for your thoughts," I said.

Nick looked at me and smiled. "A penny? After all that, all I get is a penny?"

"I also stopped by your apartment and found the flowers from the last time you were in hospital. Brought them, but forgot them in the car. Shall I have my manservant go get them?"

"Oh boy, don't let him hear that," Nick chuckled and then winced, reaching for his ribs.

I reached the side of his bed and held his hand. "So what were you thinking about?"

"Ah. I was just thinking… I hate getting shot. I hate getting stabbed. I hate getting hit by a car. I hate getting the crap beaten out of me in general. I hate…"

"Jeez, why so negative? Isn't there *anything* you like?" I asked.

"Nope."

"Puppies?"

"Worst things in the world."

"Ice cream?"

"It'll give you a heart attack in the long run."

I looked around the room conspiratorially and then tentatively climbed on the bed. Nick's eyebrows rose and he held his hands out in a semi-defensive posture. "Easy… easy… I'm still pretty… uh… tender here."

I was *very* careful when I straddled him, gently putting my weight down on his upper legs and then leaning forward until our foreheads touched. Our eyes were only a couple of inches apart and I felt his hands on my thighs, his grip still strong despite everything he'd been through.

"What about... kisses?

I held the sides of his face and lowered my lips to his, kissing him softly and then just a little harder. When our mouths parted, I opened my eyes again and let myself get lost for a moment.

"OK. I think I like those. Kisses you call them?" he asked.

I nodded. "Yeah."

Shifting my position as if the slightest wrong move might break him, I laid myself down on the side of the bed and snuggled up against him with his arm around me. For a few minutes, we silently looked out the window together.

"You have any other stalkers I should know about?" he asked.

"I'm sure I can always get more," I said.

Nick shook his head with a smirk. "That was pretty scary, wasn't it?"

"Yup."

"I love you," he said.

I sighed. How could I find the words to tell this man everything that I felt? What do you say to somebody who saved your life in every way a life *could* be saved?

He gave me back my birth mom and gave me the courage to reclaim my adopted mom. He was the one person I most wanted to see in the morning and rush back to after work in the evening. I wanted to talk to him about silly things, serious things, and all the things in between, every day of my life. Our life. I wanted to feel him with my entire body and give him mine in return.

Maybe there are no words that *really* say all that and let the full meaning shine through. At that moment, I felt like if I could actually put the full force of my emotions into speech, I might set the world on fire. I tried anyway.

With the tips of my fingers on his chin, I turned his head to look at me. "I love you too, Nick. I'm yours and you're mine, OK?"

"Absolutely."

###

Connect with me online for a FREE DOWNLOAD
Thank you for purchasing this book, I hope you enjoyed it. Please take the time to leave honest feedback in the form of a review, I very much care what my readers think and take it into consideration when planning new stories. If you'd like to drop by my website you can find me at www.emmasouth.com and sign up for my newsletter for a free and instant download of either part of an upcoming work or a short story. I'm also on Facebook and Twitter!
###

If you did like this story you may like these titles by Emma South:

Writing Our Song: A Billionaire Romance (Our Song #1)

For aspiring singer, Beatrice Hampton, the future used to be a sweet thing to look forward to, filled with the kind of joy you could write a song about. However, after losing her parents while still in high school, she is left crushed, alone, and harboring a bitter resentment towards the wealthier members of society, whom she partially blames for the destruction of her hopes and dreams. After years of lonely struggle, she can hardly remember the last time she felt happy.

That's when she literally stumbles into billionaire Jeremy Holt and things take another turn for the unexpected. Seeking only a temporary escape from the cold and grey confines of her life, Beatrice agrees to go with Jeremy on a short trip to New Zealand. On the surface Jeremy is the exact kind of man she promised herself she would never fall for but, after spending some time with him, she realises that maybe there's a lot more to the successful young entrepreneur than his money. Maybe he's the one person that can make her feel alive again.

Beatrice can't deny the spark, the chemistry, between the two of them but her past still haunts her. To be with Jeremy she must face the stresses of life in the public eye and the guilt of broken promises to herself and her parents. To be without him is almost too painful to bear. Will Beatrice and Jeremy get the chance to write the song of their love, or will they each be left with the memory of a beautiful but all too brief time when their lives intertwined?

Breaking Surface: An Our Song Novelette (Our Song #2)

Beatrice Hampton is struggling to adjust to life as the girlfriend of a handsome young billionaire. It should be easy, but when she lost her parents in her mid-teens, she lost a dearly loved piece of herself too and still can't shake that voice inside her head that tells her that her house of cards is going to come tumbling down at any moment.

This is the story of how she got that special part of herself back.

On a day that began without much promise, Bea's past and future come together unexpectedly. A beautiful memory from her youth and the love and support of Jeremy Holt give her the courage to rekindle her hopes and dreams.

Remember Our Song: A Billionaire Romance (Our Song #3)

Beatrice Holt seems to have it all. She's got a passionate and loving marriage to the perfect man, billionaire Jeremy Holt, and all the opportunities and financial security that comes with it. However, life wasn't always so wonderful. When a tragic accident results in amnesia, she is effectively transported back to a time when all her emotional wounds are still causing her intense pain. She can't remember how those wounds were healed the first time around, she can't remember her marriage, she can't remember the man behind the money at all. All she sees in Jeremy is the very kind of man she swore she would never fall for.

Can Jeremy find a way to make her fall in love with him all over again and make lightning strike twice? Can he help Beatrice remember their song or has their one chance for happiness slipped through their fingers?

45481123R00130

Made in the USA
Charleston, SC
24 August 2015